Between Two Worlds!

by

Milton H. Nothdurft

Foreword by
Brad Steiger

Published in the United States by Mountain Valley Press, P.O. Box 25432, Prescott Valley, Arizona 86312.

Editorial Consultants:
Frances Paschal Steiger
Brad Steiger
12629 N. Tatum Blvd., Suite 545
Phoenix, Arizona 85032

All portraits of Higher Beings by
Celaya Winkler
ᶜ Universal Mother Mary's Garden and the Mon-ka Retreat
116 Mercury Drive
Grass Valley, California 95945

Production by DiT0" Graphics
Dian Bonner, President
Harvey Heyder, Production Manager

ISBN: 0-9615415-0-4

Manufactured in the United States of America

First Edition: September 1985

TABLE OF CONTENTS

Foreword

As fellow seekers from the state of Iowa, Rev. Milton H. Nothdurft and I first met nearly thirty years ago. In those days, there weren't too many Iowans openly declaring their interests in awareness, higher states of consciousness, UFOs, and other things that go bump in the psyche of humankind. Through one another we met other like-minded individuals who were searching for eternal truths amidst the backdrop of the cornfields and pastures of that beautiful, but so-conservative, midwestern state.

I was always intrigued by Milt, who served one of the largest Methodist congregations in the state in a sincere and orthodox capacity, and who, at the same time, could sit up all hours of the night discussing extraterrestrial contact or poltergeists, or past lives. I never deemed his walk between two worlds as hypocrisy of any kind, but, rather, the tread of a man who was not afraid to expand the parameters of faith.

Now, after 48 years of devoted service in the Methodist ministry — Milt has authored a book of theological observations that may prove to be the most inspirational and controversial of recent times. Reared in a fundamentalist background, he early gave his life to Jesus. Now, years later, he remains as secure in his commitment to the Divinity as ever before, but he has enormously expanded the boundaries of his simple country faith.

There is no question that Nothdurft's provocative book — which openly discusses reincarnation, life after death, spirit communication, UFO contact, and psychic phenomena from a Christian perspective, will be regarded as a blockbuster in certain theological circles.

Between Two Worlds is an intensely personal book of revelation and illumination. Milt lovingly shares his quest for truth with his readers, and he does not apologize for exposing his heart, as well as his intellect. Rev. Nothdurft won his Master of Sacred Theology from Boston University and continued his scholarship at Harvard University and at Great Britain's esteemed Oxford University.

Without any trace of pretentiousness, he shares the details of his growing awareness.

Without any dogmatic assertions, he celebrates the New Age movement and the manifestation of Christ Consciousness upon the Earth.

I recommend this important new book for your premanent library of exciting inspirational volumes.

Brad Steiger
Scottsdale, Arizona

Milton H. Nothdurft

PREFACE

Many things have changed my life, my thinking, my philosophy — yes, even my theology. This has happened to many ministers as they progressed in their educational advancements.

But in my case there have been things other than educational changes, things that make my approach almost unique. I have often wondered why so many of these anomalous incidents have happened to me. "Why me, Lord?"

From the traditional changes to metaphysical concepts is almost an astronomical leap. A one-hour astronomy course in college enlarged my perception of the universe as if in partial preparation for the other changes that were to take place much later.

I was "converted" as a mere child, brought up in a fundamentalist Christian home, experienced what was then termed "the second blessing" in a holiness college. Because of the death of my mother, my grandparents provided me a home so that I could attend a state university in Michigan with its broadening influence. My college education was completed in a denominational Christian liberal arts school, Cornell College.

My seminary training began at Dubuque University, with the approach of another denomination. I met Bernyce, who would be my life partner of more than forty-five years, at this institution. A year later I enrolled at Boston University School of Theology, a liberal school of my own denomination. While there, I also attended classes at historic Harvard University, and later received a graduate degree from B.U.S.T. My wife joined me in many of these classes. Many years later we attended Oxford University overseas.

Circumstances seemed to dictate these many changes, which are perhaps more than most ministers might experience. "School spirit" might not compare with what a person would have who had gone to one school during most of his educational experience. But I believe that the broadening influence of so many different approaches was really an asset in evaluating the experiences that came to me later.

In addition, there have been trips to five continents, all fifty states of our union, to Mexico, and to most of the Canadian provinces. Three trips to Bible Lands have enabled me to hear both sides (or many sides) of the political situation of the Middle

East, an objective view that does not come to many tourists today, who hear ONE side only. Working with missionaries at their posts in South America, and twice feeling the exhilaration of being in the King's Chamber of the Great Pyramid in Egypt were widely varying experiences, but productive in their respective ways.

All these many facets of knowledge are bound to change one's thinking and broaden his concepts. But *all* of these did not open my mind as much as the lights in the sky, the "Flying Saucers," still, quiet, hovering — challenging the deepest recesses of my mind.

The UFOs had come to Waterloo, Iowa, the very week we moved there; and even as ridicule followed those who reported them, my almost immediate personal inquiries of those people convinced me that these were something not of this world. My astronomical information came in handy many times. I thought of worlds upon worlds that I knew about, and wondered how many of the stars I had learned to identify were suns with other planetary systems.

There was conflict in my mind: my astronomy course had led me to believe there could not be life on any of our planets, and that distances to even the nearest star or sun precluded travel to or from places that remote. But we had not even broken the sound barrier with our jet planes, so "slow" were we in our thinking. Our 25,000 miles-per-hour thinking was still on the planning boards at the time these things were being clocked at three to four miles per second by our sophisticated photo-theodolite telescopes. We did not have anything circling the globe (and neither did the Russians) for another ten years!

It was not *just* the "Flying Saucers," as they were called in those years, but *the way they materialized and dematerialized* right before the eyes of competent observers — and the investigation of the science behind such observations that changed my thinking beyond all former traditional education.

I remembered the words of my Lord, "In my Father's house are many mansions ... I go to prepare a place for you. And if I go and prepare a place for you, I will come again, and receive you unto myself; that where I am, there ye may be also." (John 14:2, 3) And "Other sheep I have, which are not of this fold: them also I must bring, and they shall hear my voice; and there shall be one fold, and one shepherd." (John 10:16) I was aware of several interpretations of these passages, including that of the Mormons. But was my conjecture any more out of line than theirs? Who knows *exactly* what Jesus meant?

The Masonic Lodge has a regularly-published magazine called *The New Age*. But as an approved Masonic lecturer in eastern Iowa for several years, I can truly say that most Masons do not realize at all what that means. At every lecture men who had been Masons for years would come up to me afterward and say, "I've been a Mason for years, but I never realized what was implied in some of the work as you explained it tonight!" Literally thousands of students of UFO and related phenomena have heard of "New Age" ideas as a result of their appearance in our skies and under our seas in recent years.

I recently came across a long-term sponsor of New Age ideas who is now afraid of that term because of the ignorant accusations by so-called religious "leaders," who say the New Age ideas are "of the devil." They forget that they said the same thing about Galileo and his telescope; of Madame Curié; of Lister, Pasteur, and Mesmer; and of the telephone, radio, and airplane when they first came out. Anyway, this New Age sponsor now calls his conventions "The New Space Age Convention." I have no doubt that this book will receive the same condemnation from those who really know very little about the subject!

Rosicrucianism goes into these ideas a little more plainly, as do other groups such as the Great White Brotherhood, the Yellow Hats, The Emerald Brotherhood, Summit Lighthouse, the Rainbow Focus and many others. Only spiritually-advanced members get to the place where they KNOW what is coming to pass in our world, and WHY it is not here yet. "When the chela is ready, the Master appears!"

Most Christians are unaware that the Master Jesus belonged to such a brotherhood, The Order of Melchizedek.

> *"Melchizedek king of Salem (later Jeru-salem) brought forth bread and wine: and he was the priest of the most high God. And he blessed ... Abram."* (Genesis 14:18, 19)
>
> *"The Lord hath sworn, and will not repent, 'Thou art a priest forever after the order of Melchizedek.'"* (Psalm 110:4)
>
> *"So also Christ glorified not himself to be made an high* priest; but he that said unto him, 'Thou art my Son, today have I begotten thee.' As he saith also in another place, 'Thou art a priest for ever after the order of Melchizedek ... Called of God an high priest after the order of Melchi-

zedek." (Hebrews 5:5-10)

"Whither the forerunner is for us entered, even Jesus, made an high priest for ever after the order of Melchizedek." (Hebrews 6:20)

"For this Melchizedek, king of Salem, priest of the most high God, who met Abraham returning from the slaughter of the kings, and blessed him; To whom also Abraham gave a tenth part of all; first being by interpretation King of righteousness, and after that also King of Salem, which is, King of peace; Without father, without mother, without descent, having neither beginning of days, nor end of life; but made LIKE UNTO THE SON OF GOD: abideth a priest continually. Now consider how great this· man was, unto whom even the patriarch Abraham gave the tenth of the spoils..." (Hebrews 7:1-28)

Now consider what it was that Jesus meant when he said;

"Your father Abraham rejoiced to see my day: and he saw it, and was glad." And two verses later: *"Verily, verily, I say unto you, BEFORE ABRAHAM WAS, I AM."* (John 8:56, 58)

Now this "Order of Melchizedek" is still active in our world! These masters guide political events in spite of our blunders and mistakes! When we refuse to be led by their spiritually-motivated guidance, they simply take another tack — and keep things from going completely awry! Their resources are unlimited, their ingenuity unsurpassed! Dr. Brown Landone of a former generation describes the work of this supreme spiritual order in his book *Prophecies of Melchi-Zedek in the Seven Temples,* and in other works of his.

The uninitiated are unaware of this guidance and how it is accomplished. But those who are AWARE of it are CONFIDENT of the future of this world!

The "Flying Saucers" were later renamed by our government "The Unidentified Flying Objects." Neither are accurate descriptions. And these phenomena were simply my introduction into a larger concept of the Universe, and the Omniverse, in God's Creation. It was my ENLARGEMENT OF AWARENESS far beyond what traditional education provided. Others have had their AWARENESS expanded by other "introductions." This was simply where mine began. But I am happy to say that I find thousands now who are "expanded in consciousness" to a much greater extent than a mere generation ago. Truly the "new heaven and new earth" of Revelation 21 are just around the corner. More accurately, "just around the curve," for part of it is in sight!

Later in this book we will attempt to show how all these concepts differ, and yet how they fit together. The UFOs, the secret brotherhoods, traditional religion, fundamentalism, metaphysics, the social aspects of what is happening and what may soon happen, a clearer understanding of re-embodiment for the sake of learning more about life than one could do in one mere lifetime — all this and more we will attempt to weave together in one book. I know of no other book that attempts to do this in quite the way I have discovered; which simply means that each writer, each soul is UNIQUE, and is on his own path. Any attempt to claim that any one path is the ONLY way is immoral: it violates the fundamental law of freedom of choice which was established in the Garden of Eden. There are plenty of religious leaders who are violating this UNIVERSAL law by insisting that THEY ALONE have the true interpretation of the Bible and of life!

We will also try to show that metaphysical principles were used by Christ and by his disciples in establishing His Church. Along with that we will attempt to show how some of these metaphysical or esoteric principles were removed from the teachings of the Church, and were even removed from the Holy Scriptures BEFORE THEY WERE CANONIZED. "Give me that old time religion" is a song supposing to take us back to the religion of our great-grandfathers, but the REAL "old time religion" was from BEFORE THE TIME THE SCRIPTURES WERE CANONIZED!

Many church people do not have any concept of these esoteric principles: in fact many are satisfied with a simple faith that "prayers are answered," not necessarily desiring to know HOW they are answered. That is all right, if that is where they want to remain. Every organization is right FOR SOME PEOPLE.

On the other hand, many metaphysically-minded people have given up the Church because it does not teach them enough. They are also reminded herein that they are NEEDED in the Church because of the extra knowledge and abilities which they have. I hope to speak to BOTH GROUPS!

CHAPTER 1

Once Upon A Time . . .

A S THE FIRST child of a well-liked minister in a rural parish near Detroit, I was coddled by many of the parishioners. I suppose that I remember Mr. Riemenschneider best. He had a big mustache, and his easy way of telling German folk tales had his little listener spellbound. Some of the tales could hardly be repeated for an English audience, for they had idiomatic and untranslatable phrases that were funny in German but the punch line would be lost in translation.

My younger readers will not be able to comprehend the psychological hysteria of World War I. Since we were at war with Germany, many German-Americans were suspect, and since this was a German-speaking community, they went through tremendous trauma. In the last fifty years much has been discovered about how we were psychologically "impelled" into the war. Many of the German-Americans were still receiving mail and newspapers from Germany, and the interpretations there were much different than what we were being told here. But if they tried to explain their views, people from outside the community would come in at night and throw rotten eggs on their windows, doors and front steps.

My minister-father, who preached in German at that time, had to be very careful what he said. He never was a politically-minded preacher, but even "spiritual" sermons could easily be misinterpreted, and things "read into them" which the minister did not even intend to imply! It was like "walking on eggs" to keep the eggs from one's house!

Forty years later, when my father was in the business of collecting money from alumnae for colleges, or from parishioners for church capital fund campaigns, he talked to old-timers in every major city of the United States. As a consequence, he heard many things on many subjects. Some of his prospects even told him that during World War I they were paid to perform their "patriotic duty" by producing false propaganda materials. Among these were posters that showed "those dirty Huns" about to thrust a bayonet through a baby. These were produced in this country by our own people and had nothing to do with "those dirty Huns." Such was the propaganda amidst which our loyal German-Americans had to live.

Those of a younger generation will remember our patriotic Japanese-Americans who were herded into "concentration camps" in America during the hysteria of World War II. Such are the injustices of war. And such was the background of my American parents of three generations in a German-speaking community during the first four years of my life. I had to learn English before I went to kindergarten (a German word, by the way).

The next years of my life were spent in La Porte, Indiana, and Bristol, Wisconsin, while my father got his master's degree and his seminary training — the first in the University of Michigan and the second at Garrett Biblical Institute in Evanston.

When I was eight years old, we moved to Iowa where my father had a four-point circuit in his ministry. No more student-pastorates, but he preached three times each Sunday, sometimes walking the railroad tracks when mud roads were impassable. Those were those wonderful days before pavement! How well I remember our ride to one church meeting with the district superintendent in a car with a shift lever. And when we reached the amazing speed of thirty, I wished my dad could afford a car like that!

At nine years of age, Dad let me drive the Model T Ford. There were no drivers' licenses or minimum age requirements back then. One had to watch out for stones so the tires would not blow out from stone bruises. And one had to stop for railroad tracks, for weeds were so high one could not see a train coming. There were no blinking lights!

At these crossing stops the procedures for this nine-year-old driver were not so simple. There was one foot pedal for low gear, high gear, and neutral. Neutral was half way down. That was the left foot. The right foot was the brake. If the left foot was not exactly in neutral, the car was in high gear at the same time the brake was applied for a stop. That killed the engine.

To start again was equally complex, or more so. There were

no self starters: Dad had to get out and crank. One hand lever was for gas (the right lever), while the left was for spark. The gas lever had to be down a ways, the spark lever up. But as soon as the engine started, after three or four cranks, I had to put the spark lever down, and adjust the gas lever just right so that it had enough gas to keep going but not so much as to race the engine.

Dad never complained, for he was trying to teach his young son how to drive the old Model T. But nevertheless, after this procedure happened at about the third railroad track, Dad took over the driving for the rest of that eight-mile trip!

CHAPTER 2

School Days . . . School Days

T O THE familiar tune known to all Iowans we would sing to the treetops while walking to school:

"We are from I-o-way, I-o-way,
State of all the land,
Joy on every hand,
We are from I-o-way, I-o-way,
THAT'S WHERE THE TALL CORN GROWS!"

From age eight to fifteen, my schooling was in the elementary grades and two years of high school in Hawkeye, Iowa; and I learned that we lived in the "Hawkeye State." Much later I learned that Chief Hawkeye was quite a leader in northeastern Iowa, and I climbed some of the same hills he had climbed many years before, where he had hidden from enemies.

At the end of those seven years we were moved to Colesburg. Changing schools in the middle of a high school career is difficult, finding new friends and leaving the old. But that adjustment was soon made, and I was graduated, with honors.

Returning for the 50th anniversary of our graduation was a real thrill. Only four of my classmates had died; all the rest, save one, were there. The surprise was that our principal and one of our teachers were also there. About a year later the one who had gotten us all together at his farm for this auspicious occasion was also deceased.

My folks remained in Colesburg for a few more years while I went off to college. My mother died during those years.

I have mentioned my father more than my mother, probably because I lived with him more years. But my mother was a saint, not just by my appraisal but by that of everyone who knew her in all the churches where we ever lived. Old-timers in any of those churches have told the same story.

She had borne my brother, Don, while we lived in Bristol, Wisconsin; my youngest brother, Harold, while we were in Hawkeye, Iowa. Incidentally, all three of us were born in parsonages, not in hospitals!

In Hawkeye we had a revival meeting in our church (popular in those days). I will never forget my going forward to kneel at the altar when the call was made, and having my mother immediately come to the altar to kneel beside me and pray with me. *THAT NIGHT I GAVE MY HEART TO GOD.*

Other memorable times with my mother were when she on the piano and I on my violin would play religious songs together. I had learned to play under the tutelage of a barber in Hawkeye, who was hired by the school to start a school orchestra. That started me on a long musical study, and a part in symphony orchestras in a number of the cities where my wife and I lived later, even up to the last church I served in the ministry.

Mother and I meant so much to each other that she still has, on occasion, tried to guide me even since her decease. This will be more fully dealt with in a later chapter. But I know that she still appeals to me by the music we played together and sang together as a family in my youth.

Some of this music is so old that I never hear it any more. But when it suddenly comes to my mind — songs peculiarly "hers and mine" — and stays in my mind for hours, I know that she is around! Temptations that come within the next 36 hours are things that she has seen before they happen. *THAT'S WHEN "HER" MUSIC COMES TO ME!*

Another revival meeting, this one in Colesburg, affected my religious life. I could answer more of the Biblical questions asked by the evangelist than any other youth, for which I was awarded a beautiful New Testament which I treasure to this day. In that New Testament I later got autographs of outstanding people I heard preach. One signature was that of the man who played "De Lawd" in the then-famous Negro production, *THE GREEN PASTURES.* He wrote, after I told him I was planning on going into the ministry, "Bein' a preacher ain't no bed of roses!" — a paraphrase on one of the lines, "Bein' De Lawd ain't no bed of roses."

It was this evangelist who gave me that first New Testament that was my very own, who influenced my parents and me in such a way that started my college career in the holiness school mentioned earlier. In spite of the broader education of later years, I will never regret the years spent at John Fletcher College in Oskaloosa, Iowa.

The following quotation about someone else seems *appropo* to the changing conditions in my educational and religious career. It is from *Bishop Amy Kees* by Ann Slate:

> *"She was shifted around between various family relatives. Yet in the insecurity of the many changes, she was exposed to numerous houses of worship, and so the chains of one dogma did not encircle her. Amy's concept of God expanded past the trappings of a solitary religious doctrine."*

Some of the greatest changes in my life came during college and seminary, which could be said about almost any well-trained minister. But there were many other features which changed not only my educational thinking but my emotional stabilization as well.

I was brought up in the simple faith of simple church people at a time when not many laymen had any theological education of any kind. They just believed "The Good Book" for what it said. The "liberals" believed in the "social gospel"; the "fundamentalists" in the "personal gospel." It bothered lay persons that there was "politics" in the church, just as among politicians. Lodges and Service Clubs have the same "politick-ing" before elections of their officers. But it just does not seem proper in the church. And the "fundamentalists" blamed the "liberals" for the "politics" in general church meetings. My father was caught in the middle of this struggle, at a time when "evolution" theories of Charles Darwin were adding fuel to all the other argumentation that was going on.

While most of this was beyond me at the time it was happening, we young people were having our own arguments. Methodists, Baptists, Presbyterians, and Catholics were debating things they didn't understand very well themselves, but *each* was sure his ideas were right and the other kid's arguments were wrong. Mormons, Blacks, and Indians were not to be found in northeastern Iowa or that would have added another subject-matter to the debates. We had enough to keep the conflagration going! At least drugs and booze parties were not prevalent in high schools in those years. Sex was a topic of conversation, but intimate encounters were limited to "French kisses" and "petting" more than in today's world — unless you want to tell me that I was in a "protected environment" and didn't know what was going on!

I went away to college — a "holiness" school where we had a week of revival meetings each semester — praying for those "who had not received the second blessing." Holiness meant "complete sanctification." This was the "perfect love" which John Wesley hoped to "attain in this life." This was constantly preached, but not always "lived," I'm afraid. I went home for vacations, doubtful that my own parents had ever received the "second blessing."

This attitude in my own mind at that time was a foretaste of the judgmental attitudes I found in many parishioners later in my ministry, especially when the "charismatic experience" or the "speaking in tongues" movement became for many people the criterion of the really true and dedicated Christian. I began to wonder how many more experiences I must have in order to be sure of my salvation. I learned my lesson, and got beyond that insecurity in my theology. I just wish thousands of other judgmental Christians could get beyond their hang-ups!

My mother died in my third year of college, and this changed the lives of the whole family. In fact, most of our lives after that were lived in four different states, although my younger brothers lived with Dad under varying circumstances for several years yet.

Mother's funeral was in Ann Arbor, Michigan, where my German Methodist minister-grandfather and his wife lived, after their retirement from the ministry. They owned two houses in which they had apartments which they rented out to Michigan University students. "Mama and Papa Bau" had other children in Ann Arbor and Detroit.

Dad discussed with the whole family just what he expected to do after this shocking development in our lives. To help solve some of our problems, my grandparents offered me a small room in their apartment house so I could finish my work at the university. I found a job at a boarding house for my meals that next year.

Imagine my chagrin and disappointment to discover when I registered that instead of being a senior I was a second semester sophomore! The grades in Bible and other courses were not acceptable at a state university. So I studied one year and a summer there, when I was told by my grandparents that they could no longer afford to give me that room for another year.

The feeling at a state university was certainly different from the college campus where we had a curfew at night, no cards, dancing or even movies allowed. Those who sneaked out a window to go to a movie were severely punished. I have often wondered what that school does now about TV rules, where the movies are even more explicit than were the theater movies of those days!

I went to the University of Iowa where things could not be worked out in time for the fall semester. I tried Cornell College. This attempt was successful, thanks to the dean of men, Albion Roy King and his wife, who gave me a home in their basement for certain chores around the house, and where I was helped to find a church in Solon, ten miles to the south. I had had a church during my third year in college. To this second church I rode a motorcycle every Sunday. In extreme weather a local taxi driver took me for a very small fee.

My horizons were being broadened through experiences in a "holiness school," a non-religious state university, and a Methodist college. I was graduated from the latter in 1936.

After some disheartening experiences with a housekeeper who did not make my brothers feel comfortable in their own home, my Dad went to Oregon in the summer of 1936, probably in an attempt to "find himself" in a peaceful environment. My brothers were being taken care of by an aunt and uncle for the time being. Three of my friends and I decided to drive out and join him. We found him in a cherry orchard, picking cherries for a living. We joined him. The other three fellows found other work after cherry-picking season, and Dad and I wound up selling vacuum cleaners!

On our way back to Iowa, Dad and I stopped at beautiful Mt. Hood. We decided to climb it. Dad gave out 1200 feet from the top, and told me to continue. I made it to the top, almost exhausted. Being inexperienced at mountain climbing, we hadn't realized the distance involved and hadn't eaten for three meals by the time we got down. But from the top I saw "The Three Sisters" a hundred or more miles away, an unforgettable experience. Dad has used this as an introduction to his sermon on "Biblical Mountain Top Experiences" many a time. I believe this was the beginning of my love for the mountains, and why I live in the mountains in my retirement.

Back in Iowa we visited friends in Hawkeye.

That night Jesus appeared to me just as plainly as if I had been with him in Palestine after his resurrection. Whether it was a dream or a vision I cannot be sure, but to me *it was real.* He hovered above my bed for some moments, just beyond the foot. He was not standing, but hovering in the air.

Whether he spoke or not I cannot be sure, but of this I am positive: the peace I had at that time was a peace I cannot adequately describe. And, unlike many dreams, it is as vivid today as it was in the fall of 1936. He seemed to assure me that all was well, and that he would be with me always. That same peace comes whenever I recall that "appearance."

There are ever so many people, including ministers, who do not see God's guidance through people. I recall bitter feelings by many lay persons and clergy during my youth over "disappointments in appointments." The bishop "appointed" a man to be their minister whom the congregation did not like even before he got on the scene. And ministers were heard to say that "this is God's church, but the appointments are made by the bureaucracy of the cabinet, or the autocracy of some bishop." And starting with that attitude, they didn't get along in that charge. If they had accepted the appointment graciously, who knows how the Lord might have blessed their efforts in that charge! That is why I make the following point.

When Dad and I got back to Mechanicsville, his appointment for that year, I received a telephone call from a district superintendent that neither of us particularly liked. He asked me whether I would take the Guttenberg church for the coming year. It had been left "without appointment" at Conference time. The reason was that the man who had preached there for seventeen years had been elected as President of the University of Dubuque. In order to assume that responsibility he had to become a member of the Presbyterian Church.

I told the superintendent that I didn't want a church: I wanted to go to seminary in Boston, where a pal of mine from the "holiness school" was now in attendance.

The D.S. said, "You could go to a seminary in Dubuque while preaching at Guttenberg." After a long conversation he requested that I think it over and call him the next morning.

The next morning I hadn't changed my mind, but I called him, as I had promised to do. I don't know yet how it happened, but over the telephone he "twisted my arm" until I agreed. I was two weeks late in registering, but the seminary was understanding and let me in.

I now firmly believe that God used this district superintendent for several reasons: 1.) I did not waste the year; 2.) I had the enlarging experience of spending that time with students and professors of another denomination (predestination was one of the points of argument in my high school days); and 3.) toward the end of the school year I met my life partner, Bernyce.

The guys in the seminary were compatible, predestination was not talked about as I had expected, and we had fun together. They helped me park my motorcycle, helped me fix it when necessary, were interested in the Guttenberg church, and generally made life enjoyable for me. I enjoyed the professors, the library, the town, and the rides up through Millville and along the beautiful Mississippi River to the old river town of Guttenberg.

It was my future wife's senior year, and my *only* year at the University of Dubuque. Eight months of that school year had gone by before Bernyce and I had our first date, through the influence of my roommate. Again God was using a person to help two people find each other for life.

When it has been so plain in my own life, it is hard for me to understand how many people never see God's will being done by means of common ordinary people.

There are changes that bring about God's will for some people through a personal vision or psychic experience, and that will be dealt with later on. But for the most part *people* play a great part in helping God's will be done, even if they are unaware at the time that they are instrumental in so great a decision for another whom they have influenced.

The next year I did get to go to Boston University School of Theology, where the friend from the "holiness school" had found me a job working in a restaurant. Here I earned the exorbitant sum of $4.95 a week and one meal a day for working two hours a day, five days a week. That bought my other meals and paid laundry bills!

That year I looked for a church again. In May I was promised one, for the following fall. That enabled me to get married June 9, 1938. I hitch-hiked back to Bernyce's home in Iowa and we were married by her minister and my father in her church — the LeRoy, Minnesota, Presbyterian Church. Dad let us use his car for the honeymoon, which consisted of the journey to our first job together, via Niagara Falls, of course.

Cherry Valley was a suburb of Worchester, Massachusetts, and since there were other student-ministers nearby, I shared a ride with one of them when Dad needed his car in the fall. I stayed in a seminary dormitory four nights a week, doing my preaching and calling on week-ends.

The new bride found herself doing some painting in the parsonage while I was gone, and we worked together doing garden work in the summers. We hitch-hiked together to New Hampshire and Vermont, and later to New York City for short vacations, something we would not try now!

Those were frugal years. Our total yearly salary was $1000.00. Each Monday the treasurer came by with the Sunday collection, usually between $18.00 and $19.00. Every month or two someone had to go around to individuals to ask for more — "to make up what was owed to the preacher." In spite of a busy schedule, we did get invited out to meals sometimes. We had no washer and no dryer, not even a wringer. Clothes were cleaned on an old style washboard. Sheets were wrung out by having my wife on one end and I on the other, and *twisting* until damp. Our radio was our one luxury!

But prices were different then, too. The trolley went right past our house. It cost five cents each way and took us the two miles downtown. On Friday afternoon our celebration of being together again consisted of getting to a matinee before six o'clock so we could get in for twenty-five cents. At the White Tower hamburger place, we could eat for a quarter (ten cents for a hamburger, ten cents for a piece of pie and five cents for a glass of milk). We also shopped for groceries for the coming week. We would come home on the trolley with two *big* bags full (a week's supply) for $5.00! We wonder how young couples today would fare under similar conditions, to which they have never grown accustomed!

I was in seminary in Dubuque, Iowa one year, in Boston seminary (alone) one year. We were together in the East two years. My third year at Boston was spent in getting a Master's degree in theology, with a major in social ethics.

My formal education lasted more than twenty-two years. This is counting kindergarten, elementary and high schools, three colleges and universities, two seminaries, classes in Harvard Univeristy and Oxford University. In the latter we studied under the translators and editors of the New English Bible (first "authorized" version since King James').

All this diversity, as I have stated, meant I had little "school spirit" as people usually refer to it. But on the other hand it gave me a multiplicity of views — a combination of many different perspectives.

One thing I was taught by several of these schools was "to think for yourself." That's what I learned to do, and that's what I do in this book.

Those who are confined by one, or a very few, viewpoints will probably not be able to go beyond Part I. But Part II is simply a continuation of a process that was thrust upon me by circumstances — or "planned by Higher Powers!"

INTERPLANETARY SPACE CRAFT. Picture taken Feb. 26, 1965, sent to me by a friend, Mrs. Madeleine C. Rodeffer of Silver Spring, Maryland. This picture is very much like those sent to me by George Adamski before the publication of his books. At a time when "authorities" were saying "Show us some pictures, if there are any," pictures like those taken by many friends of mine were already in distribution among early investigators. Denied as authentic by the "authorities," we knew the photographers and had no reason to believe them fakes. Thirty some years later, I still believe these friends of mine who gave me their personal pictures, over the "authorities" who have lied over and over to the American public.

CHAPTER 3

The Advent of the Flying Saucers

I T HAS SEEMED to my friends as though I fit into the sign of Aquarius all right (my birth sign, along with my father's and one brother's). One friend, a Leo with an Aquarian wife, and still another friend with an Aquarian husband used to celebrate our Aquarian birthdays together. The non-Aquarians always joked about what a life they led with these Aquarian spouses!

Even before I got into the study of metaphysics, I was extremely diverse in my interests. I studied piano with my pianist-mother, which was not easy. However, it gave me the musical background to get a start in many other things — singing and playing.

We went to a local concert in a town of 500 where a traveling violinist played, I guess it was on the Chatauqua Circuit. In my youthful imagination, and from the distance I was sitting, the hairs of the bow *seemed* to be going right through the strings of the violin. I was fascinated! I wanted a violin.

A local barber was musically-inclined and had just been hired to start a school orchestra. This was before music and art had much place in school scheduling. I took private lessons, and from such meager beginnings I got to play in several high school orchestras — and finally in a Boston orchestra while I was in seminary, and in two symphonies, in Waterloo, Iowa, and in the Sioux City Symphony.

I sang in the only male quartet in any of the high schools that I attended. Later I sang in choirs in two colleges and two seminaries. One of these was the Boston University Seminary Singers who took a singing tour of the east coast, and the next year sang about ten days at the Uniting Conference of the Methodist Church in 1939.

Other hobbies started with a one-hour course in astronomy in college that my roommate talked me into taking. I think that one semester hour has helped me more than any other course I ever took! In the first place it certainly enlarged my concept of the universe in which I lived! This was perhaps another step in the "enlarging" mind concept that has constantly kept me growing. I just cannot understand people who don't have anything to do or who have no interests once they retire. Life has probably just begun for me at seventy! The wonderful thing is that I know now that one never *loses* anything. We can keep on growing, learning, and progressing *even after we die!*

Another way in which that astronomy course helped me is when the saucers came to Waterloo! I had watched the phases of the moon, learned many of the constellations, knew where the planets were most of the time, and knew when Venus was a "morning star" and when it was an "evening star." So when the "authorities" told us that a flying saucer was "the planet Venus" that someone had mistakenly called a saucer, I knew that they were purposefully lying again, for Venus was not in that part of the sky where the saucer had been sighted. It has also helped me straighten out some people who *thought* they saw a saucer because I knew it *was* the planet Venus! I know of no planet which has so often been mistaken for a saucer as Venus, partly because it is so brilliant and partly because people in general do not realize that it changes from an evening star to a morning star in just a few months — and then back again to an evening star.

Of course, planets are not really stars. But there *is* a star that rises in the northeast that seems to be *moving back and forth* at times. I have been called on the telephone innumerable times to "go out and look at so and so, in such and such a place," only to find out that it is either the planet Venus or the star that has fooled me, too, at times. It *seems* to be moving back and forth because of the air currents. It is similar to, but not exactly like, the "bent visual rays" when one looks at a boat oar in the water, seemingly bent, or when one looks at the pavement on a hot day and sees the movement of the heat rays coming up off the pavement. Like a mirage also, it is an illusion. But because these things *do* happen so often, the "authorities" have gotten away with their "explanations" of *real* UFOs by calling them illusions, or hallucinations, or weather balloons, or "freaks of nature" like "sun dogs" on either side of the sun.

Yes, my having been "talked into" taking that one-hour astronomy course under a young professor who made it really a fun course has helped me in many ways. Many times I wonder whether this guidance really came from "upstairs," using my roommate to get it done. If there was any really important reason for my getting so involved in a serious study of the UFOs and related subjects, then the "planning" must have started 'way back in my early years of education.

As John Burdon Sanderson Haldane wrote, "I suspect that there are more things in heaven and earth than are dreamed of, in any philosophy."

We often received news of UFOs in other nations, where governments released the information (or the Catholic church in Rome, with the cardinal's "imprimator" on the cover) — but that *never appeared in the United States.* People often say, "You can't tell me this news wouldn't come out, as many free lance reporters as there are roaming around all the time and everywhere!" What they don't seem to realize is that "reporters don't print the newspapers!" And many people are not aware of the pressures on the publishers that do!

My reading has been quite diverse, in an attempt to learn what is *not* in the newspapers, the magazines, radio, or TV. My diverse interests have been in many fields — scientific ("borderland sciences"), political, economic, "patriotic," psychic, reincarnation, UFOs, Masters of the Far East, the "Lost Ten Tribes of Israel," and many others. The latter subject has been researched by hundreds of writers in just the last hundred to two hundred years (they *were* "lost" until then)! Three of the most powerful propaganda groups in the world are not happy about this information, so they have more of an influence on teaching in the seminaries than any of us realize. We miss the "Kingdom Message" thereby.

Certain people want us to think that the Jews are *all twelve tribes of Israel,* and they even named their new country "Israel," a misnomer if there ever was one! But a careful study of all the evidence that has been discovered in the last one hundred or more years would convince most people of its authenticity.

If you are one who believes "the authorities" without question, you will call this a "cult." But if you think for yourself and "search the Scriptures," you will learn that the Lost Tribes have many more people in them than does the Jewish community, and that they fulfill the prophetic promises more accurately! For forty years I have discovered that they can foretell more accurately than any other prophetic group the exact dates on which some world-changing events will occur (although they do not say what those events are going to be). But sure enough, when that date rolls around, something that changes the course of history, some decision that is made, does happen on that day.

Another world-wide group to which the Lost Tribes information is not happy news is the Roman Catholic hierarchy. They do not like the world to know that the first Christian Church outside Palestine, Asia Minor, and Greece was in England, not in Rome! Joseph of Arimathea was a wealthy owner of tin mines near Glastonbury in Somerset; and after the persecutions began in Jerusalem, many of the disciples went with him or followed him into France and England! Together they founded a Christian Church in Glastonbury on the island (at that time) of Avalon. The legends and traditions there are still strong!

The evidence that would have proved it was destroyed in the Protestant-Catholic wars that went on during the time of Henry VIII and following monarchs. But the proof is all over the world in the prophetic promises that have been fulfilled by these people, and by their enemies who have conquered half the world in this century, and who are also mentioned in the Bible.

The third large group that has succeeded in keeping the "Kingdom Message" from being accepted are the Fundamentalists! In emphasizing "personal salvation" almost exclusively, they have left out the important fact that God established His Kingdom on Earth at Sinai, which has had *continual existence* ever since. It did *not* cease with the Judean king, Zedekiah, but was in existence, with a king of the lineage of David on the throne, *elsewhere* at that very time.

The United States of America, established by a reincarnation of the prophet Samuel, is very much a part of the Ten Lost Tribes of *Israel!* The entire Bible has a whole new meaning and is very much up-to-date, when one interprets it not only in terms of personal salvation, but in terms of God's Kingdom on earth! With all the sixth century deletions, "Personal" and "Kingdom" salvation are still there.

Another reason for our not hearing about the migrations of

the *real* "Israel" in the last 2500 years is the very essential difference between Protestantism, Roman Catholicism, and Jewish scholars.

In the May/June 1982 issue of *Biblical Archaeology Review* (official bi-monthly organ of the Biblical Archaeology Society, Washington, D.C.) an evaluation of Biblical archaeology in America states that ". . . was — and still is — largely a Protestant affair."

Gus Van Beek, curator of Old World archaeology at the Smithsonian Institution in Washington says, "American archaeological efforts in the Holy Land have been dominated by Protestants, both clergy and laymen."

The editor of B.A.R., Hershel Shanks, gives the following statistics: "Almost 70% of our members are Protestant, 15% Catholic, and only 10% Jewish. Most people are surprised to learn what a small percentage of our readers are Jewish. Probably fewer than 20% of synagogue libraries subscribe to B.A.R."

The article goes on to give the reasons for this difference in each case. The reason for the Protestant domination of American archaeology in the Holy Land lies "chiefly in the nature of Protestantism itself; it is Bible-centered and has been Bible-centered since the Reformation."

If it is the Protestants that are the most interested in the diggings going on in Bible Lands, where much of the history of the Israeli people took place, it is just as logical that it would be they who are most interested in following the Israel peoples through their 2500 year migrations through the Caucasus, Russia, Germany, Scandanavia, Britain and America!

The "Lost Tribes" (the *real* "Israel") constitute many times more people than the Jewish peoples of the world.

CHAPTER 4

Speakers and Space Brothers

IN 1954 BERNYCE and I went on our first pilgramage to the Holy Land. We had begun a Club some years before to study the UFO phenomena. It was one of the first saucer clubs anywhere, as far as we knew then. We still have not heard of one that began earlier. We called it the "Cup and Saucer Club." We always had coffee and lunch, and we studied "saucers"; therefore, the name. We published one of the first UFO periodicals, called the *Round Table*.

When I say "we" began the Club, I do not refer to my wife and me alone. There were several interested parties, one of whom I call my "mentor" in all the various fields of study which follow. We have become lifelong friends, always keeping each other informed on many subjects. This Club is still meeting every month, having been in continual existence for well over thirty years!

But it seemed *something changed* after our Holy Land Pilgrimage! Speakers began coming through eastern Iowa as though they were also on a pilgrimage! They came from many states — New Jersey, Maine, Florida, Michigan, Illinois, Arizona, California, and others. It seemed to be a constant stream for several years!

It got to be a laughing matter when an old maid, who was "snoopy" in many other ways too, started driving by every time we were holding one of these meetings. The funny thing was to see her stop, get out a flashlight, paper and pençil, and write down all the license numbers on the cars that were out front, and drive on down the street. It *was* perhaps the *only* house in town where, every time there was a rather large meeting, there was always a license plate from a different state! We had reason to suspect she reported to someone else in town.

I finally had to have a meeting with my bishop about it. After his mild suggestion that I "stick to the gospel," I told the group, and we simply decided to meet in other towns. The speakers continued coming as usual, but our snoopy friend could no longer report on our activities, for she did not know when or where the meetings were from that time on! She has now gone to her reward, as has the bishop.

Some of the people in the saucer field that spoke to us were Howard Menger, Dana Howard, George Hunt Williamson, George Adamski, Robert Coe Gardner, Buck Nelson, Frank Stranges, John Otto, Rheinhold Schmidt, Charles Laughead, Willard and Eunice Quennel, and Dick Miller.

But we got into other fields of research. There were things about the saucers that could not be explained from principles of physics which we know. Sudden "appearances" and "disappearances," not "flying" toward people, or away from people, but just "suddenly being there" or "not being there." They were like ghosts appearing and disappearing. Another thing hard to explain was when people would estimate the speed of a UFO at upward of a thousand miles an hour, suddenly making an *acute angle change of direction!* Not a wide curve, as our airplanes would have to do to change direction. How could anyone survive the G force of such an abrupt change, *if* there was anyone in it at all.

UFOs would appear on pictures that were taken of other things, although no saucer had been seen at the time of taking the picture. Or the reverse, trying to take a picture of a saucer, which did *not* appear on the picture, although everything else was there. And *most scary of all*, a lone person on a lonely road would take a picture of a saucer at night. In a day or two a "man in black" would come to the person's own house, demanding to be given the picture, although the picture-taker had not told a soul that he had done so. Only a person *on the saucer* could have known!

A valedictorian of his class in Jefferson, South Dakota told of lights that he saw in the road ahead of him, for which he slowed down, because they seemed to be in the middle of the road.

When he was almost upon it, it raised in the air, went over his car, and disappeared *as a mist*. We were invited to his party after his graduation, and his teachers corroborated the fact that they had gone out to the road after this happened, at his insistence, and saw marks on the cement road which indicated that some object of *tremendous weight* had sat there and scratched the lines off the road when it arose!

Two other things top off this story. His family had seen *two* UFOs eight hours before this, *over their farm,* signalling each other by light flashes — although this was several miles from where the thing had landed *just before he got there.* Was there a connection between the two sightings, involving the same family? How did "they" (upstairs, in the UFO) "know" that this was the same lad over whose farm several miles away they had signalled each other eight hours before the landing incident?

The other thing I learned that night was that this teenager had already given a lecture to the Junior Academy of Science of South Dakota on the subject, "Extra-terrestrial Life." Did "they" know that, too, and was that why they "appeared" to him? Needless to say, I have followed this lad rather closely in years following this incident!

Another incident that got us into other studies was when Ric Williamson was with a group from Winslow, Arizona, having radio contact with the "Space Brothers." They had turned their *transmitter off,* but left their radio *receiver on.* They talked about having a picnic. On the *receiver* came the suggestion they go to a certain place in California. They contacted George Adamski. Then followed the famous meeting with the "man from Venus," after which Ric made a plaster cast of the alien's footprints in the desert.

How did the Space Brothers hear the conversation about having a picnic? E.S.P.? Or is their equipment so sophisticated that they really do not need the earth group's transmitter to hear their conversations?

Incidentally, when we returned from the Holy Land we had stopped in London at the apartment of Desmond Leslie, nephew of Winston Churchill. He was co-author of George Adamski's first book. As we were having tea with him, we noticed some plaster casts on his mantle. They were the same plaster casts that Ric Williamson had made in the desert in California. If, as some say, George Adamski dreamed up this whole story, why would the nephew of Winston Churchill have thought it important to have those plaster casts on his mantle in his London apartment?

Another subject of our studies started with the green fireballs in the Southwest. I wrote personal letters to Dr. Lincoln La Paz, a famous astronomer who was studying them carefully. We later heard from him about the subject; and from other sources (he dared not endanger his reputation), we learned that the saucers were putting them into our atmosphere to clear out the radiation that had been left by the above-ground atomic tests in Nevada (and maybe White Sands, New Mexico?).

Here was the beginning of the world-wide ecology push — to clean our land, water, and air which we had polluted so terribly. Soon our above-ground atomic tests ceased! Rachel Carson became so well known for her *Silent Spring* that as I write these lines in 1984, her picture appears on some of our postage stamps.

Don't say "the saucers have gone away; one doesn't hear of them anymore," when such tremendous strides have been taken *by earth man* as a result of things they were pointing out to us in the fifties and sixties! We are *trying* to keep the air a bit cleaner with catalytic converters on our cars — though some are aware that we need to do more in this line, for we are spewing out other gasses just as dangerous.

Atomic Energy indeed is revolutionary. But that drew the attention of the saucers — the dangers inherent therein! The *fire* of the atomic bomb made us aware of the other elements of Ancient Wisdom — *air, earth,* and *water!*

Neva Dell Hunter, one of the lecturers, told us that most of us would be in the Great Southwest in a matter of time — and here we are. Three fourths of our group have moved to New Mexico, Arizona, and California within a quarter of a century.

The reason is perhaps similar to the reasons Brad Steiger gave when he wrote about "Why So Many Psychics Are Moving To The Southwest." As I recall, it has something to do with the vibrations of the land here. They "feel" it when they drive through.

I know one sensitive who came to Prescott, Arizona, saw a beautiful "aura" over the town, and stayed several weeks, giving lectures and lessons by simply putting an ad in the local paper. Another psychic came to Arizona from California and was working with the police helping to solve crimes for several years before returning to California.

One psychic walked into a church and saw the person he had been "directed" to come to help sitting in the choir. The person he was to aid is a daughter of a colleague of my wife's in the Sioux City school system, who now also lives in the Phoenix area.

The visiting psychic walked up to this young lady after church services and plainly said, "I have come to help you. I was directed to do this." The young lady had had such a bad case of psoriasis most of her life that she had to wear high-collared blouses, long sleeves, and could never be seen in shorts.

The minister and choir joined him in "prayer," and by evening the infection she had had was gone, and the psoriasis was gone in a few days — and is still gone!

This "gift" has its tragic side, too. A psychic that I knew in Waterloo, Iowa sometimes could "see" an accident that was about to occur. These things can be avoided if people pay attention to the warning. The accident is not inevitable!

But this psychic plumber walked up to a couple in a booth in a restaurant and said several times that they should not "go out onto the road tonight." They just laughed, and ignored the warning. They ended up that night in a very tragic accident on the road.

The psychic told me, "Such a 'gift' is not always a blessing. Sometimes it is a curse. You don't know how it hurts a person to 'see' some tragic thing that is about to happen and not be able to do a thing about it, because of the unbelief of the persons you are trying to warn!"

If more people were aware, and "believing," much tragedy could be averted! But instead, well-meaning people, *especially* some church people, say "such things are of the devil," and therefore continue to foster tragedy in the world that could be avoided!

Jesus said it so well, but many Christian people don't listen to Jesus. He said, "If I cast out demons by the power of Beelzebub, then his house is divided; and a house divided against itself cannot stand." Some Christians can't seem to see the obvious logic of what he said!

Another phase of the "Speakers' Parade" through Iowa was when we were introduced to the Spiritual Frontiers Fellowship (SFF) by Neva Dell Hunter, mentioned earlier. The organization was but a year or two old, but has been gaining in influence ever since. It was designed for the purpose of studying *survival after death*, *spiritual healing* and its mechanics, and *prayer* and how answers to prayer are sometimes brought to pass. It went beyond simple faith, and was attempting to help faith by *knowledge* of how these truths can come into our lives. It was an *aid* to faith, and for many people it made faith stronger! Some church people said, "I thought I believed in life after death, for the church has always taught it; but there was always a bit of fear until I started studying these things. I am no longer afraid at all!"

I attended the second and third national conventions, and I was soon asked to be one of the speakers. My topic was "How to Start a Study Group." SFF later made copies available. Many groups were started all over the country, and finally seminars sprang up, attracting as many people as the national annual meetings.

My topic was patterned after the schematic of our eastern Iowa "Cup and Saucer Club," telling how to begin, stick to the same time (people would finally adjust their other schedules to fit), end on time, have refreshments afterward, and then visit after the program if any wanted to stay. We had discovered that people *grew* in many ways simply by the association with other interested people studying similar things. People who were "on the frontiers of such study" often felt "alone" in their interests. But when they had occasional contact with others who were like-minded, they didn't feel so isolated in their search, and the very psychology of that association released powers within them they hadn't realized were there!

I was elected to serve on the National Executive Committee to fill out someone's term, and later re-elected, so that I spent seven years on the National Executive Council, for which I received a certificate of appreciation.

Spiritual Frontiers Fellowship was patterned after England's The Church's Society for Spiritual and Psychic Studies, and there were many contacts between the two groups, including Reginald Lester coming to this country as a lecturer, and several psychic "healers" and renowned "exorcists" who had "cleared" many "haunted" places in England and elsewhere. So the "Speakers' Parade" continued!

In this field of research we discovered quite a few people who had had "Out Of Body (OOB) Experiences," some of which were actually "death experiences" where they experienced the glorious exhilaration of what the after-life is like, only to be met by a "Light Being" and told that this was not their time to "come over." They must return to earth, for their mission there was not completed. To those who enjoyed the experience so much that they wanted to stay, the Light Being would have to appeal to their emotions by reminding them of a wife, husband, or chil-

dren who still needed them and who would be very greatly hurt
if they did not return. These people (at least those that I have
met) invariably have completely lost their fear of death, and are
usually involved in some philanthropic activities to help others
besides just their own families.

We have also met many clairvoyant and clairaudient people
(some at SFF Seminars, and some just personal friends) who
actually could 'see' in the aura of a person just where "dis-ease"
of the physical body was, and could "direct their psychic energy" to that spot where it was needed. Or they would name the
"doctor teacher" who did the psychic healing from another
level of awareness (we would call it "the other side of the veil").
So this study turned out to be not only a "help to people's faith,"
but an actual healing of the physical body by a "healing of the
etheric body, or aura."

I mention this for the sake of those who think "Mysticism is
not practical, but only visionary." I also mention it to remind
the reader of how our thinking, feeling, acting, *and ministry*
changed as a result of our "beginnings" with Unidentified Flying Objects research!

I am thankful to God that I have been guided to see the good
and the bad in our world, and that I have been able to *maintain
my faith* in the Ultimate Triumph of Good Over Evil! To see
only one side or the other is either hopeless pessimism or blind
optimism. My attitude is not a pollyanna simplistic approach,
but a reasoned optimism in spite of possible horrors, because of
the many positive, constructive, other-worldly information that
has also been provided me!

If I knew *only* about "Saucers," I would be "gullibly serene";
if I knew *only* about the hate-and-fear-filled people who are
afraid to let go of the Piscean Age, I would be afraid of tomor-
row. *I am neither.*

There may be trials to go through for all of us. Some fundamentalists enjoy seeing the horrible killing going on in the Middle East, "because it shows the nearness of the Second Coming
of Christ." If they were only *more Fundamental* than that! The
Christ is coming again, and has already been seen "in the
clouds of heaven." But if they also knew how the Christ-consciousness is coming in the hearts and thoughts of millions of
Aquarian Age people, *they would be scared out of their wits* —
because they can't understand what we mean, or how this mystical power operates!

And the Liberals, or Modernists, are just as hopelessly unaware of what is happening! In a constant barrage of Social Activism, they think that if they could only convert the world to their way of thinking, the problems would disappear. Though I preached it for ten years of my ministry, it now appears to me as a "Works" kind of faith. More "works" than "faith."

In spite of a fundamentalist background and a liberal education, I have grown beyond them both. I say this not in a judgmental attitude or an attitude of superiority, for I have learned that each person has a separate path to the goal — and this is the path my Leader has led me into. *You* should take the path *your* leader leads you into — but not with a closed mind! Open up to *all* the things going on, and accept only what is *right for you!*

JESUS THE CHRIST whose vibrations were raised after his crucifixion to the Higher Realm where he was not limited to time or space, but suddenly appeared to as many as 500 disciples at a time, sometimes in a room closed and locked for fear of their enemies! Many Space Commanders (the "hosts of heaven") of these Higher Vibrational planes speak most respectfully of him, and are under his command in this Grand Plan of the Ages! He appeared to the author in the fall of 1936.

CHAPTER 5

Still Another Enlightenment

I N MY YEARS in the National Council of Spiritual Frontiers Fellowship, I was sent as a delegate to the Association for Research and Enlightenment (A.R.E.) and became acquainted with many of their leaders. Hugh Lynn Cayce, son of Edgar Cayce, was always present, and everyone always enjoyed him — in Virginia Beach, and wherever he held seminars in the country. We sponsored him in our Sioux City church at a morning worship service, and later for a group that became interested in the 14,000 Edgar Cayce readings.

I will never forget the ideas he brought forth about "How to Remember Your Own Past Lives." He suggested that one think about 1) the historical novels you have enjoyed most (where were they supposed to have taken place, and when?); 2) the historical movies you have seen that have most impressed you (not the plot but the place!); 3) if money were no object, where would you most like to go and spend some time? (not just from something you have heard about the place, but desires from your inntermost being); 4) besides the American food you are used to eating, what kind of food do you like the best — Chinese, Mexican, Indian, French, German, Greek, etc.?; 5) besides the race into which you were born, or the country, what nationalities or races of people do you most enjoy associating with?

These may be *faint memories* which you have never before interpreted as having any significance. Any one of them might tell you a whole lifetime you spent in that environment; or better still, if several of these faint memories seem to indicate the same place, or the same kind or group of people, you might start examining other things about that race or nationality to see what other memories might be brought forth.

I will always remember one person in one of my churches who

was particularly taken with me, and I with him. There was no "church" explanation for that affinity, for he was not "religious" and neither did he get involved in any church activities except my sermons. He became interested in our "Saucer Club," and soon became its president. He assimilated easily most of the ideas expressed there.

As time passed, his job took him away from Iowa, and he moved to California. Because of this affinity, he kept inviting us, and several times we were in his home there. We were close to the whole family. He began to have feelings that we had lived together before. After a long time it came out that *if* swords were used now, he would know exactly how to use them, and would be ready to, in *my* defense, if it ever became necessary *again*.

Again? He was sure that he had been a Roman soldier and had *defended me* during the Roman persecutions of the Christians. He had admired my beliefs, *and my stand*. It became clearer to me why he was always so interested in my sermons, even though the church, as such, was not that important to him. But I became his "father confessor" on more than one occasion.

Once we had gone together to a medical doctor near Maquoketa, Iowa, who was using hypnosis to help mothers in their child-bearing. We discovered that privately he was also interested in past lives. So my friend persuaded the doctor to hypnotize him. Not only did we discover that he had been a cowboy in the lifetime just preceding this one (he always wore cowboy attire in this lifetime; now we knew why), but we also learned how he died, and where, and under what conditions! He had died defending a young woman who had been exploited by a man of unsavory character. The former had walked into a bar, been shot in the back, and died with his face in a pool of his own blood on the barroom floor!

The woman was back in this lifetime too, living nearby, married to a wonderful man — and the two families were good friends. My friend recognized the connection immediately. And we have *all* been good friends ever since.

Now this brings me to a conclusion, *and a warning*, that I think should be included here.

Many people in the metaphysical realm (but not only there) have been immediately enamored by someone of the opposite sex, and a marriage was broken up thereby. They sometimes have *recognized* someone they were very close to in a past life, and mistook it for love.

Not that it isn't, sometimes. Dr. Gina Cerminara studied the Edgar Cayce readings, receiving her doctorate in psychology for her work in this field. Her book *Many Mansions* includes passages that indicate that sometimes people will have completed the "karma" with one particular spouse, the arrangement of that marriage having been made before coming to earth. They then take up with another, to complete "karma" with a second person in the same lifetime, which arrangement was also made before coming to Earth. This puts an altogether different light on divorce.

In these cases, possibly the other spouse in the first marriage remarried a person with whom he/she also had other karma to take care of. So the long-run result is not *sadness,* but *two-fold joy* for all four (or more) persons!

But here is the question — and the warning: How does one know that one made such arrangements before this life began? "The other woman," or "the other man" might be a *temptation,* instead of a *former lover!*

Is it a deep spiritual attraction, or a mere infatuation and desire of the flesh? Is this (first) partner one with whom I will have to make further adjustments because of some of my own weaknesses, and had I better stick with this one until we get *everything* settled? If there are children, what will a sudden change do to them (a *most* important consideration)? If I am simply "enamored" with this second person, how will I get myself extricated from this involvement? If I *do* marry this second person, and it *was not* in the original "arrangement in heaven," have I multiplied *my* karma *and* his/hers by succumbing to what I thought was love? And a still greater dilemma: can a person "truly love" two persons at once? And if so, under what conditions — married and mistress, or what?

The Warning is that one had better be *very careful* in simply thinking "this is someone from a former life" and therefore "we ought to be together." This is a greater danger in the metaphysical field where reincarnation is accepted as a matter of course, than it is among fundamentalists, although it happens there, too.

In light of what Hugh Lynn Cayce said in regard to how to learn (without an Edgar Cayce around) where, and under what conditions, one lived before, I acknowledge at once that one doesn't *have to know!* Maybe I'm better off not to know all my past. Why drag around the memories of many lifetimes, when we have enough garbage in this one?

One possible answer is simply to learn where certain problems came from. I have had many courses in psychology and some approaching psychiatry. While the ego of some psychiatrists is so strong that they will sometimes prolong "therapy" for years — rather than admit that they just don't know the answers — there are an increasing number of psychiatrists and psychologists who are treating with hypnosis and other means. "Regression" has been used more and more in recent years. Psychologists are discovering problems that originated in early childhood and even in the womb! And a few brave ones are regressing patients into "life before conception" and even former lifetimes.

The main purpose, as I see it, is that if and when the patient can learn *when* the problem originated, and *under what circumstances,* he can more easily deal with it himself *in this lifetime.* There have been cases where the patient discovers that *in this lifetime* the conditions no longer exist under which this problem originated. And when *consciously* accepting this fact, the problem is solved!

I have a definite feeling that many allergies which people have (and I live in the midst of an abundance of them in Arizona!) *might* originate in some innate fear that came from a former lifetime, and that if they could discover *when,* and *under what conditions,* that fear began, the allergy would also disappear — without medication!

Then there is another advantage — that of knowing what one ought to be doing, especially in times when work is hard to find. In many cases of people who came to Mr. Cayce for a reading because of a deep disillusionment with their life as it was going, they discovered that if they would change employment (the *kind* of thing they were doing), they would be happier, and more effective.

In some of these cases, the inquirer discovered that he did some particular kind of work in a former lifetime — and *did it well.* When changing to that *kind* of occupation in this lifetime, not only were the persons happier in their vocations, but in some cases actually became millionaires because of it.

But becoming a millionaire should not be the object of one's search! Mr. Cayce himself almost lost his gift at one time because of such materialistic pursuits. When he realized that this was a *spiritual gift,* and that it should be used *for spiritual growth purposes,* he was able to help thousands of persons.

The Source of Edgar Cayce's readings was from a Universal Store of Knowledge. He and Nikola Tesla and a few others had been involved in many lifetimes of helpfulness on this planet and others, therefore tapping into this "Universal Knowledge." Then came the steady stream of *Unidentified Flying Objects* which gave us more information and inventions in those fifty years or so than this planet had received in thousands of years previously.

Let me digress here long enough to say that often when I give my "U.F.O. lectures" at noon service clubs, I run into questions afterward such as: "What do you mean we have been 'given' some of these technical advantages by Space Brothers? I'm an engineer, and I know the process by which transistors were evolved over many years of research."

Then they are all so anxious to "get back to their business in five minutes" that they don't want to wait the fifteen more minutes that it would take to answer that question! Materialism has such a hold on them that they have already forgotten that the phenomena that I have expounded upon "could not be explained" by *physical* principles that we now understand.

Also they have already forgotten that I said that miniaturization of parts (which made our space program possible) was *preceded* by ten years of UFO activity before any nation even put a satellite in orbit! (Sputnik went up and over our heads in 1957, and our first satellite not until the next year. The Flying Saucers were *internationally* publicized by the Kenneth Arnold incident over Mount Rainier in 1947. But they had been around for years before that, we later found out!) And there had been earthly *contacts* long before 1947!

Of course "they" do not "make a transistor" and place it *intact* into the hands of earth scientists on a given day! They are experts at E.S.P. (Extra Sensory Perception — and Projection), as I pointed out in the Williamson-Adamski experience in the early fifties. I knew personally at least *three* witnesses to that meeting!

No — "they" put *ideas* into people's heads that had *not* been put there by earth knowledge before that. Sometimes that knowledge was so different that only the *brave* scientist would try it! But it worked! Just like some of the very *unorthodox* treatments that Edgar Cayce suggested *always* worked — if the patient followed the directions to the letter! Then, at a later time, other "suggestions" were put into someone else's mind, which that person *added to* the ideas he had heard some unorthodox scientist had tried — and it worked also. So *gradually* the miniature devices were "evolved," as my engineer friend in the audience had said. But he had not given me the time to explain *how* these gifts were given to earth scientists. We have all heard of *inspiration;* but we seldom think of it in these terms, or realize *from whence it came!*

I have just about decided *not to lecture to noon clubs at all any more.* If they do not allow me *one hour* for lecture and questions. I am through with their exasperating questions for which they do not really want the answers — because they think they know the answers already!

George Adamski wrote a final book stating that his Space Brothers had informed him that they had tried to work with the leaders of the world (I know of one president and two queens who were *vitally* interested in the fifties). Since that effort was unsuccessful, then they would change their tactics for so amateurish a society as we have. They would *help us get out into space,* and then *we would see for ourselves* that there is life out there. And they have done just that! And *we have seen their life on the moon,* but the officials will not tell the people. (Canadian broadcasters, I am told, have broadcasted messages from astronauts on the moon to Houston and Houston's answers to them — "because they had no obligation to NASA to keep quiet!")

Maybe the reason is not so obscure when one remembers what I said about *who controls* presidents, kings, queens, parliaments, congressmen and the media. Someday *the truth will out!*

CHAPTER 6

The "Star of Bethlehem" and the "new Jerusalem (City Foursquare)"

SEVERAL TIMES I sponsored lectures by George W. Van Tassel in Sioux City, Iowa. He had worked four years as a flight mechanic for airlines at Chicago and Cleveland. In 1930 he was employed by Douglas Aircraft in California for 8-1/2 years. He went to work with Howard Hughes in 1941. Later he went to Lockheed Aircraft at Burbank for 4-1/2 years of flight test work there.

In 1947 (the "year of the saucers," mentioned before) he leased the abandoned government airport at Giant Rock, a place that came to be known world-wide for his nearly twenty years of "Flying Saucer Conventions" there. Many phenomena showed up, visually and on cameras, at that spot; and George himself was visited one night and taken aboard a ship. His book, *Into This World and Out Again,* was copyrighted in 1956 and is one of the classics of that era.

Another classic of that era is Trevor James' (he later added "Constable") book, *They Live in the Sky,* copyright 1958, in which the author lists a number of the abductions of people and even airplanes by UFOs. We have long known that there are both the Guardians of our planet and the Invaders, those working for the Light and what are known as the "dark ones" or "dark forces." Light and Dark have been acknowledged in most of the religions of the world, so this is nothing new. The main difference is that those from another dimension have, on occasion, become visible, and there have been visual sightings of UFOs "swallowing up" an airplane which was never seen again.

The Borderland Sciences Research Association under Meade Layne had the etheric (other dimensional) explanation of "flying saucers" as early as any other "explanation" ever given. This is now the Borderland Sciences Research Foundation, carried on by Riley Crabb out of Vista, California. Mark Probert also gave this etheric explanation while in a higher than normal state of consciousness.

Now these three sources (and others) have referred to "Shan Chea," which means in our language "Earth-child" satellite, which has been orbiting our planet "for almost 2000 years, since the appearance of Jesus the Master upon your surface." It is reported to be 1500 miles square (sic!). The scientific attitude has been that such statements are pure balderdash and properly belong in the science fiction field.

However, the information regarding these satellites (there are two more) was on record before astronomers Dr. Tombaugh and Dr. LaPaz located the so-called moonlets, and may be the reason these gentlemen began looking for them. Until their location, astronomers were quite sure there was no heavenly body closer to earth than the moon. Even Dr. LaPaz and Dr. Tombaugh could not "see" the moonlets, which were alleged to have been detected by radar. According to George Van Tassel, these space stations are "positive to light," and therefore not visible to our positive polarity vision. (*Note* how this corresponds to the Biblical passage I will refer to in just a few paragraphs!)

I had correspondence with Dr. Lincoln LaPaz at the time of the "green fireballs phenomena." We saw several of these ourselves, some falling *lightly* to the ground just ahead of our car one night in Iowa, and one that was travelling horizontally just ahead of our car in Missouri (at least five witnesses in our car). Without endangering Dr. LaPaz' reputation as an acknowledged astronomer, I can say that our correspondence definitely indicated to me that not only was he looking for an answer to the green fireball mystery, but that he was looking for *something big!*

I saw something in a syndicated article in the newspaper, released by one of the agencies of our government, that there was a satellite circling our earth *from East to West!* This was a mystery to them (though the general public might not understand why at that time) because what Cape Canaveral (before its change of name to Cape Kennedy) was sending up were all going from west to east! Nothing from east to west!

So here, from a government release, was a "leak" (?) about something that was entirely different from anything we had sent into the skies! They deny the existence of Extraterrestrial ships, and yet are *constantly* leaking information like this that only the alert reader will see and remember!

So here are astronomers looking for something *big,* the government releasing information about an "Earth-child" satellite they cannot explain, and people with either clairvoyant abilities or actual contact with Extraterrestrial Beings explaining its size and characteristics!

Now go to your *Holy Bible* and search various translations of Revelation 21. This was a "vision" given to John the Clairvoyant (called "the Beloved" in the Bible).

Here is the description of what many fundamentalist Christians believe is heaven, with pearly gates and golden streets. Yet the second verse clearly states that it will come *down* to earth *from God* and *out of Heaven.* Furthermore, it will be *visible to human eyes* — "a glorious sight" *(The Living Bible).* The *Home of God* is now among men, and *all things will be made new,* which is what modern Extraterrestrials have been explaining to hundreds of channels for the past forty years! This is the "New Age" or "Aquarian Age!" And the time is *soon,* according to modern testimonials from many "contactees" with Other Dimensions!

Note in verse 16 that the dimensions of this Holy City, the "New Jerusalem," are 1500 miles square — the same dimensions as modern clairvoyant or contact persons have reported to us in recent years.

Other comparisons: from Ashtar — "It is a complex assemblage of instrumentation which permits constant surveillance of your surface and the beings upon it." *(The Lamb's Book of Life)* (Nothing evil will be permitted in it — verse 27 — although its gates never close — verse 25). "Shan Chea will pass through the atmosphere of Shan (Earth) and a great commotion will be caused by its appearance. It will be visible to physical eyes at that time." (The glorious sight of verse 2)

Much of this information comes to us from Ashtar, commander of one of the main ships in this gigantic fleet, and who has been giving constant messages for many decades. We have a picture of Ashtar, painted by a clairvoyant artist, and he is quite different from any picture of Jesus I have ever seen. Yet these various commanders are loyal to Jesus the Christ and are working in complete harmony with "the Father of Lights," the Creator, at all times. We know from Jesus' words in the Bible that enemy spirits "tremble" at the word of Jesus! Some of them in his incarnate life on earth said, "Have you come to torment us *before our time?*" They, too, know their time is short!

I am quite aware of the unethical abductions by "the Invaders," or "Dark Forces," the "Men in Black" and other names. But since I gave my heart to God at that altar very early in life, I have not changed my allegiance to him who is the Author of Life. I have persisted in a life-long study of the Bible, which I honor as the "Word of God."

What I have said in this book is *not* in contradiction to anything I have found in the Bible. It only augments my understanding of many things in the Bible that are vague to many people.

Jesus said he was going to prepare a place for us who *thorouhly* believe in Him as God's Son. I have seen with my own eyes — and my family has seen — some of the vehicles by which I hope to be transported from this three-dimensional world to that more perfect dimension where "in the twinkling of an eye" we shall be "changed," as many people have already experienced, and *have come back to tell us about it!* They still have work to do; they are the "forerunners" of what we "believers" can expect to experience, even as those who have had the death — and out-of-body- experiences that show them the glories of that dimension where beauty, music, love and fellowship are indescribable on this plane — except as we see the exuberance and entire lack of fear on the part of those who have experienced it and returned!

The Bible clearly defined the "good spirits" and the "bad" and tells us to "test the spirits." *We know which side is going to win, so we do not fear!*

CHAPTER 7

Jesus Taught Reincarnation

IN EARLIER PARAGRAPHS we mentioned that religions, except for *western* Christianity, believe in reincarnation. In our studies we discovered that Jesus taught it, too, and later we found out *who* removed most references to it from the Bible, and *when* it was removed, as well as *why*.

But the culprit who removed this spiritual teaching missed some significant verses. One such passage is as plain as daylight if one reads with an open mind:

The disciples Peter, James and John had been with Jesus on what has been called "The Mount of Transfiguration." One might also note the psychic reference in this passage, as Jesus was talking to two men who had been dead hundreds of years — Moses and Elijah, and so sure was Peter of it that he wanted to build three places for them up there, "one for thee, and one for Moses, and one for Elias (Elijah)" (Matthew 17:3, 4). They must have materialized rather plainly for Peter to think of building "three tabernacles" out of physical material!

The disciples were so impressed by the psychic experience *and* the "transfiguration" of Jesus that Jesus had to admonish them, "Tell the vision to no man, until the Son of man be risen again from the dead." (verse 9)

Many of us learned in the early years of the fifties that one "tells no one" of some of the things one experiences — or they treat one as if he were demented! While one still does not blurt out these sacred experiences to just everyone, it is *very much more acceptable to students of mysticism now* — and there are thousands more of such people than thirty-five years ago!

Surely the "Aquarian Age" is very close, if not indeed actually here! *Time is on our side!* "The time is now," as so many "Star Persons" have reported to Brad and Francie Steiger.

The strange thing seems to be *why* Peter, James and John at least did not comprehend what Jesus foretold about his "rising again from the dead," after having had *this* experience with "dead men!"

But going back again to the passage in Matthew 17, we see that the disciples *did* seem to comprehend that *this man was the Messiah!* After all, it was Peter that just a short time before this had replied to Jesus' question, "Who do *you* say that I am?" — "Thou art the Christ the Son of the living God." (Matthew 16:15, 16). It is my firm belief that Jesus would not have allowed them to have the "Transfiguration Experience" *until* after they comprehended *who he was!*

So the Malachi passage in their own Scriptures (chapter 4, verses 4 through 6) occurred to them on their way down the hill:

4. "Remember ye the law of Moses my servant, which I commanded unto him in Horeb for all Israel, with the statutes and judgments.
5. Behold, I will send you Elijah the prophet before the coming of the great and dreadful day of the Lord:
6. And he shall turn the heart of the fathers to the children, and the heart of the children to their fathers, lest I come and smite the earth with a curse."

So the disciples asked, "Why then say the scribes that Elias (Elijah) must first come?" (verse 10 of chapter 17)

To which Jesus replied, "I say unto you that Elias (Elijah) is come already, and they knew him not, but have done unto him whatsoever they listed. Likewise shall also the Son of man suffer of them." (verse 12)

And as if this verse were not plain enough, Matthew adds this one: "Then the disciples understood that he spake unto them of John the Baptist." (verse 13)

John, if you will remember, was beheaded by King Herod, at the behest of a dancing girl who pleased him at the feast. And Jesus did not begin his ministry until *after* this horrible thing had happened to John. So John had died at the instigation of his enemies, just as Elijah had killed the prophets of Baal in King Ahab's time. Was Herod a reincarnation of King Ahab? Or a re-embodiment of one of the priests of Baal? Jesus said to a man in the Garden of Gethsemane, "Put up again thy sword into his place: for all they that take the sword shall perish with the sword." (Matthew 26:52)

In John, chapter 9, is recorded the story of a man who was *born* blind. The second verse indicates the widespread belief in karma — "Whatsoever a man soweth, that shall he also reap." (Galatians 6:7).

In the second verse of John 9, the disciples ask, "Master, who did sin, this man, or his parents, that he was born blind?" Now think that through: most people don't give that question a thought at all. The assumption was that if the man was born blind, *someone sinned* — either the man himself, or his parents. Now *if* it were the man himself, *when did he sin? Before he was born? He was BORN blind!*

An altogether different ending is given in *The Aquarian Gospel* by Levi, who it is said "read the Akashic Records" to compile this whole gospel, which also includes many things about the "unexplained 18 years of Jesus' life not found in our Bible." It might be enlightening to you to read a copy of that gospel, as recorded by Levi Dowling.

Is this puzzling question in verse 2 and its aftermath another instance of a teaching that was changed in the sixth century? But they forgot to change the *implication* of the question, which any thoughtful person wonders about. Sometimes I think we have heard the gospel stories so often and they have become so old to us that we quickly pass over many things without thinking. Someone once said, "Many people have just enough Christianity to immunize them against the real thing."

"Levi" was a scholar in his previous lifetimes. he dictated *The Aquarian Gospel of Jesus The Christ* through Levi H. Dowling from the Akashic Records. The name Levi was given to him by his parents without their knowledge of the work that was before him. Below is quoted from the *Aquarian Gospel* the story of the man born blind, his healing by Jesus, and a beautiful interpretation of how the man's karma was taken care of in a more productive way than normally:

> "And Peter said, 'Lord, if disease and imperfections all are caused by sin, who was the sinner in this case? The parents or the man himself?'
>
> And Jesus said, 'Afflictions all are partial payments on a debt, or debts, that have been made. There is a law of recompense that never fails, and it is summarized in that true rule of life: 'Whatsoever man shall do to any other man some other man will do to

him.' In this we find the meaning of the Jewish law, expressed concisely in the words, 'Tooth for a tooth; life for a life.' He who shall injure anyone in thought, or word, or deed, is judged a debtor to the law, and someone else shall, likewise, injure him in thought, or word or deed. And he who sheds the blood of any man will come upon the time when his blood shall be shed by man. Affliction is a prison cell in which a man must stay until he pays his debts *unless a master sets him free that he may have a better chance to pay his debts.* (Emphasis mine.) Affliction is a certain sign that one has debts to pay.

'Behold this man! Once in another life he was a cruel man, and in a cruel way destroyed the eyes of one, a fellow man. The parents of this man once turned their faces on a blind and helpless man, and drove him from their door.'

Then Peter asked, 'Do we pay off the debts of other men when by the Word we heal them, drive the unclean spirits out, or rescue them from any form of sore distress?'

And Jesus said, 'We cannot pay the debts of any man, but by the Word we may release a man from his afflictions and distress, and make him free, that he may pay the debts he owes, by giving up his life in willing sacrifice for men, or other living things. Behold, we may make free this man that he may better serve the race and pay his debts.' " (Chapter 138:3-17)

CHAPTER 8

The Early Church Fathers Accepted Reincarnation, Too

WE CANNOT GO into all the teachings of the early Church Fathers, but a few brief quotations might help us to see that reincarnation was a part of early Christianity, *until expunged by the Fifth Ecumenical Congress of Constantinople in 553 A.D.* I will quote from at least four who were not laymen, but *Saints!*

Origen (born in 185 A.D.) upheld the doctrine until his death. According to the *Encyclopedia Britannica,* his ten books of *Stromata* have disappeared leaving almost no trace. This is of paramount significance, in that Origen occupied himself here in correlating the established Christian teachings with the "Christian" dogmas of Plato, Aristotle, Numenius and Corrutus.

Origen states in his own *Contra Celsum:* "Is it not more in conformity with reason that every soul, for certain mysterious reasons, is introduced into a body according to its desserts and former actions? Is it not rational that souls that have used their bodies to do the utmost possible good should have a right to bodies endowed with qualities superior to the bodies of others?"

And in his *De Principiis:* "Every soul . . . comes into this world strengthened by the victories or weakened by the defeats of its previous life. Its place in this world as a vessel appointed to honor or dishonor, is determined by its previous merits or demerits. Its work in this world determines its place in the world which is to follow this."

It is important to respect the distinction these worthies made between metempsychosis — the dilatory migration of souls through sub-human shapes — and a series of progressive rebirths in human form.

St. *Jerome* (340-400 A.D.) once impulsively hailed Origen as "the greatest teacher of the Church since the Apostles." This is hardly plausible if the New Testament was then as ambiguous in its references to reincarnation as it is now. Surely for Origen to have held pride of place among the Early Church Fathers for nearly four centuries his tenets must have been based solidly on what at that time were accepted as the true gospels.

St. Jerome also asserted, "I think a divine habitation, and a true rest above, is to be understood: *where rational creatures dwelt, and where, before their removal from invisible to visible, they enjoyed a former blessedness.*"

St. *Clement of Alexandria* (150-220), in his *Exhortation to the Pagans* is also influenced by Plato, as were the others. "We were in being long before the foundation of the world; we existed in the eye of God, for it is our destiny to live in Him. We are the reasonable creatures of the Divine Word; therefore we have existed from the beginning, for in the beginning was the Word . . . *not for the first time does He show pity on us in our wanderings; He pitied us from the very beginning.*"

To St. Jerome's and St. Augustine's views on Plato must be added those of St. *Gregory* (257-332), who affirmed that "it is absolutely necessary that the soul should be healed and purified, and if this does not take place during its life on earth, *it must be accomplished in future lives.*"

St. *Augustine* (354-430), held Plato in such veneration that he writes in his *Contra Academicos:* "The message of Plato, the purest and the most luminous of all philosophy, has at last scattered the darkness of error, and now shines forth mainly in Plotinus, a Platonist so like his master that one would think they lived together, or rather — since so long a period of time separates them — *that Plato was born again in Plotinus.*"

To come full circle, Plotinus (205-270), was a fellow-disciple with Origen under Ammonius, who founded the famous Alexandrian School of Neoplatonism in Egypt in 193.

Here we have the testimony of *four Saints* — not laymen, but *Saints* — of the early Church. They cannot *all* have had bees in their bonnets; nor would they have embraced beliefs that were hostile to the contemporary tenets of their own church. They repeatedly refer to the "Christian" dogmas of Plato; so they obviously subscribe to the belief that Christ had included them in His own philosophy.

Let me add to this list of *Saints* the name of *Pythagoras* (582-

507 B.C.). Diogenes Laertius, one of his biographers, quotes him as asserting that "he had received the memory of all his soul's transmigrations as a gift from Mercury, along with the gift of recollecting what his own soul, and the souls of others, had experienced between death and rebirth."

No wonder Pythagoras has been immortalized by so many people, and has given us so much to live by even all these centuries later!

My wife and I well remember the day we were riding in the back seat of someone's car when our three-year-old daughter said several things that absolutely amazed us. They were things an adult would not even dream of, let alone a three-year-old!

We said, "Anita, where did you ever hear such a thing?" Her answer surprised us as much as what she had said in the first place: "I heard that in heaven, before I came here."

Alas! Most of us forget, or were "talked out of," some of the things that *we knew before we came here.* But there are *faint* memories all of us have, and we have discussed them for the sake of those who may "want to remember."

What has sometimes been called the "Parable of the Pounds" (Luke 19:11-27) has often been interpreted simply as the different number of talents we all have. Each is rewarded according to what he has done with the talents (or pounds) that were given to him, when "the certain nobleman" returned from "the far country" to which he had gone "to receive for himself a kingdom, and to return." How few interpret this as Jesus Himself being "the certain nobleman!"

When he returns, he rewards everyone according to what he has done with that which has been given him. But the one that did *nothing* with what he had been given was also rewarded — but his reward was not so good!

But notice what Jesus includes at the end of the parable. When He (the "certain nobleman") returns, he says, "Unto every one that hath shall be given; and from him that hath not, even that he hath shall be taken away from him."

But as if that were not enough of the lesson, he adds: "But those mine enemies, which would not that I should reign over them, bring hither, and slay them before me." (verse 27) If reincarnation is a *fact of God's Law,* then are those same members of the Sanhedrin who were so filled with hatred for him going to be around to receive the kind of "reward" (the law of cause and effect) mentioned in verse 27? It appears that we are soon to find out!

CHAPTER 9

Karma of the Now

I WOULD LIKE to discuss a little different aspect of the subject of reincarnation since its distortion and almost complete absence from the current fields of law, medicine, politics, sociology, finance, psychology and religion are responsible for much of the trouble, crime, and war in this world. Reincarnation needs to be re-emphasized — almost over-emphasized — so that the world comes back to its senses and provides justice and mercy in all other fields!

Francie Steiger, wife of Brad Steiger, has had continual contact with a real angel from childhood. She has been subject to the Psychological Stress Evaluator (PSE) tests, and is probably one of few psychic-sensitives who has ever passed such a test. From her book *Reflections From an Angel's Eye* (copyright 1982 by Francie Steiger, used by her personal permission) I quote:

"Nearly all of the world's great spiritual teachers, prophets, and religious leaders spoke of Karma, for they taught of Divine Justice, the law of cause and effect. Those of us in the Western Hemisphere are more familiar with the teachings of Jesus, and perhaps you may recall his speaking of reaping what one sows. Or you may remember, "And they that take the sword shall perish with the sword ... What you do not want done to yourself, do not do unto others. (The Golden Rule in reverse. Author)

"Certain religious teachers have sadly believed that precisely whatever you do on Earth that is wrong will only be done to you in Hell. Others have thought that the sins you have committed in one lifetime will be dealt out to you in another, new life experience. For example, if you strangled someone in one lifetime, that victim or another individual, will have his chance to strangle you in the next, though you would most likely have no idea why you met such a fate. Logically, of course, this would create a cycle that would have to be perpetuated with your getting even with him in the next go around. And even if it were not the exact victim getting his revenge on a perpetrator of injustice, this interpretation of Karma would always require one who executes the just punishment deserved, and he would then become the 'receiver' of it in the next life. There would be no end to this form of justice. This was a misinterpretation of an eye for an eye and a tooth for a tooth syndrome. The justice we reap for those energies we create is immediate; we will either elevate or lower our vibrations on every level of our being, mentally, physically and spiritually."

My wife and I have seemed to notice in the last twenty or thirty years that justice has been meted out very soon to people who have very evidently violated the Law of Good. We wondered whether "the time was so short," as many people have noticed, that there might not be another lifetime in which to correct this lifetime's errors before the Great Catastrophe that is to cleanse the world.

The Space Brothers have often told of this cleansing that is so close, and they have even created and brought here Great Space Cities, encircling the Earth at a tremendous distance, but with the "disc craft" that come to Earth from the Mother Ships from time to time. When our family has seen some of the effects of misdeeds so soon after the miscreant has performed them, we have a family joke that calls this "instant karma," though this really is not funny! But Francie's explanation continues:

. "That which I have received through my channeling of the angelic teachings has told me that those who oppose the Divine Plan of God are those who will reap chaos in equal measure to that which they have sown. And they will reap what they have sown in the NOW! They will be affected by their chaos as soon as it has been created and gathered into their electromagnetic vibrational field. And the effect that they have engendered will be felt on every level of their being, lowering and bringing havoc to the frequencies of mind, body, and spirit.

"Be advised, therefore, that through our lack of awareness, through our denials of the truths of God's Plan, through our discordant interactions, we, ourselves, can be affected by our trespasses against others. We can be disharmoniously affected by our created and gathered energies. When we oppose the Divine Plan, the Christ Vibration, we chaotically affect our total self. Mentally our 'sins' will bring about emotional imbalances, neuroses, attacks of anxiety, and great stress. Physically, our systems receive those chaotic energies, and our body becomes weakened or imbalanced in various ways, and we become susceptible to various illnesses or diseases. Spiritually, our vibrations are made chaotic, distorted, and the energies of our spirit, lower. We therefore make ourselves more susceptible to seduction by those entities of the lowest realm. When this occurs, we also run the risk that upon the death of our physical shells, our low-vibrating spirits within will most certainly blend and join those of likened, distorted energies, in the place commonly known as Hell.

"Depending on your awareness and your understandings, you have the ability to reverse so many discordant conditions in your life experience. You have the ability to create and gather harmonious energies of the highest order. Through contact with the Realm of Highest Vibrations, through interacting with your angelic beings, by reflecting your Soul in your daily life, and by living in accordance with the Divine Plan of God, you can control all that can affect your spirit and your mind, and that will result in the affectation of your body."

Think, then, of the different interpretation of law that would occur if we go back to the teachings of most of our religious teachers, including the Jewish Kaballa and the Christian Bible!

If a person "hears voices telling him to kill someone" and he commits the act, the person is given psychological tests — or on the advise of a psychiatrist — is deemed not responsible "by reason of insanity," and goes free of the murder penalty. He may be given treatment and turned back on the streets to continue his nefarious practices, because his *spirit* has not been cleansed from the "seduction by spirits or entities of the lowest realm" An alcoholic draws the spirit of a former alcoholic, now deceased, to himself, and after a crime "doesn't remember having done anything" — and *he* gets by on "temporary insanity!"

English and American law has often been connected to Jewish law, and is said to be based on the Bible. *Which Bible?* The one that *leaves out reincarnation?* Or the one *before the time of Justinian and Theodora?*

There are people who can "read the Akashic records" and could tell us exactly what was in the original Bible. But alas! the hosts of evil see to it that psychic gifts are ridiculed to the extent that most people would not believe it if they saw it!

Witness almost every television movie that has a psychic in it, and you will almost always see that by the end of the movie the psychic has been revealed as a fraud who is "conning someone out of his life's earnings!" I'll wager that the producers of that type of film *are the ones making money hand over fist by their misinterpretations of the Laws of the Heavenly Hierarchy!* Their karma is overdue.

But without elaborating further on my views on the subject, I will say that every week in the news I *see* the karma of that *misinformation* coming to fruition! It *is* happening, just as Francie's angel said it would happen, *in the now.* (Only I wouldn't dare tell *to whom this is happening* for fear of reprisal before these truths get to the public, so world-wide and intricate is this system of evil!)

Universal Mother Mary
Blessed Among Many Women
"Goddess of Motherhood"
© 1979 by Universal Mother
Mary's Garden and the Mon-
Ka Retreat, 116 Mercury Drive,
Grass Valley, California 95945.
(Artist · Celaya Winkler)

CHAPTER 10

God **Outside** *of Me or God* **Inside** *of Me?*

A T ONE POINT we discussed the difference between looking outside of oneself for God or looking within. I wish to emphasize that difference: it just *may be* that that is the difference between "orthodox" religion and many "metaphysical" concepts.

Let us not assume that one is right and the other wrong. If *both* are right, then there is a point of confluence of the two! Again let us use the imperfect example of the sparkler and the sparks. The sparks would not be there if it were not for the sparkler; but the sparkler is not the *all,* for there *are* the sparks that emanate from the sparkler!

There are the orthodox that just cannot see God as anywhere except *out there somewhere,* even though the Scriptures tell us that we were made *in the image* of God! But maybe *looking within* is not the only place to look for God either. It was fashionable among one group to say to each other, "The Christ in me sees the Christ in you." If we really believe that "God is everywhere," then there is no place that God is *not!* "Whither shall I go from thy spirit? or whither shall I flee from they presence?" (Psalm 139:7-12)

But there is more to this simple evaluation than meets the eye! There was a great difference between "orthodoxy" and the "gnostics" in the first century or two of Christianity! Essentially, the conflict existed because of the relationship between politics and religion. Some of the Church Fathers did not see the difference as we do today. If God was the heavenly ruler, and had given complete authority to his earthly representatives, then politics and religion were one, and everyone in the "catholic" faith should accept the authority of His representatives. This "discipline" was a part of "being a Christian."

On the other hand, the gnostics had a different attitude about "authority" and "discipline." *Agnostic* means literally "not knowing"; those who *know* about ultimate reality are *gnostics* ("knowing"). *Gnosis* involves an *intuitive* process of knowing oneself; and *knowing oneself*, one *knows* God, and is not subject to earthly authority. If one *really* "knows" oneself, self-knowledge is knowledge of God; the self and the divine are identical.

This was anathema to the bishops, probably jealous of their power and authority over the Church. Clement says there are bishops, priests, deacons and laity, in that order — just like the hierarchy of heaven. And whoever refuses to "bow the neck" and obey the church leaders is guilty of insubordination against the divine master himself. Whoever disobeys the divinely ordained authorities "receives the death penalty!"

The Gnostics, on the other hand, had a very different structure of authority. They demonstrated that, among themselves, they refused to acknowledge such distinctions. Each time they met, they "drew lots" for the role of *priest*, for the *bishop* who was to offer the sacrament, for the one who would *read the scriptures*, and for those who would address the group as *prophet*, offering extemporaneous spiritual instruction.

The next time the group met, they would throw lots again so that the persons taking each role changed continually. So even the distinctions established by lot could never become permanent "ranks." And most important, they intended through this practice, to remove the element of human choice. This was not considered "random choice" as moderns might call it. They believed that since God directs everything in the universe, the way the lots fell expressed his choice! This is typical of some parts of Old Testament beliefs.

Valentinus claimed that besides receiving the Christian tradition that all believers held in common, he had received from Theudas, a disciple of Paul's, initiation into a "secret doctrine of God." Paul himself taught this secret wisdom, he says, not to everyone, and not publicly, but only to a select few whom he considered to be "spiritually mature." Valentinus offers, in turn, to initiate "those who are mature" into his wisdom, since not everyone is able to comprehend it.

So these "spiritually mature" considered themselves above

domination by human authority (clergy). And the "orthodox" considered these as rebels to divine authority and called them "heretics."

Is this the distinction today between those who still accept the authority of the Church, and those who "turn within" to find their "divine direction?" And which is right? Or is it possible that *both* attitudes are still needed, depending upon the individual's spiritual maturity and understanding?

But neither should be dominant! Each has its own place. And as long as this planet is a schoolroom for learning, *all* must try to understand the other, and live together in peace!

Those of us who received our theological education before the 1940's heard about "the mystery of the gospel" (St. Paul) and the "mystery religions" which may or may not have influenced both Paul and John in his gospel. References are in *The Interpreter's Bible,* which was written and published soon after World War II. In 1954 I visited both the King's Chamber of the Great Pyramid and the ruins of the Eleusis labyrinth in Greece, both of which have been said to be initiation places for "the mysteries." One of these, it is reported, is still being used for Rosicrucian (and maybe Masonic) work.

But in 1945 there was found in Upper Egypt an extremely important find by an Arab peasant. Named after the town near which it was discovered, it has been known as the Nag Hammadi Library. This whole subject is discussed in detail by Dr. Elaine Pagel (doctorate from Harvard) in her book *The Gnostic Gospels* (Random House; copyright, 1979).

Again, it was scholarly rivalry and jealousy that largely account for the long delay in the public exposure of these 52 texts, some of which may be older than the New Testament gospels of Matthew, Mark, Luke, and John. The reason for the popular interest is the new light the Gnostic Gospels throw on the nature of Jesus and his teachings, the status of women, the nature of God and the opposition to what became the orthodox institution of the Christian Church.

While most reviews of the book have been highly favorable, it has also been attacked, largely by those who believe the Bible should be accepted in the literal meaning of its every word. The Gnostic Gospels interpreted Christ's life and teachings in symbolic rather than literal meanings. In light of our *present* controversy about the status of women in the orthodox church, not only in Roman Catholicism but also in Protestant ordination of clergy, and the difference between clergy and laity, it seems the Gnostic-Orthodox question still is not settled!

Will I be dismissed as "obsessed with a single idea" if I point out some more anomalies between all this and the flying saucer mystery? Or is there a single plan for bringing out ancient truth in many ways at this critical time in history? And all beginning at approximately the same time?

The value of the Nag Hammadi Library became clear when the French Egyptologist Jean Doresse saw the first of the recovered manuscripts *in 1947* at the Coptic Museum in Cairo (which is near the Great Pyramid). This is the same year that the Dead Sea Scrolls were discovered also "quite by accident," near the Qumran Essene settlement. Both were discovered by Arab peasants. Scholarly jealousy entered into the release of both.

This was also the *Year of the Flying Saucers,* released to the world by international news services after Kenneth Arnold saw the nine disks near Mt. Rainier. Some of the Dead Sea Scrolls are in a new and famous library in Israel, built *since* that date *in the shape of one of George Adamski's Flying Saucers!* (I remember from personal first-hand knowledge how terribly interested the Jews of eastern United States were to have George Adamski come and speak to a large group of them at a special meeting.) This "Adamski picture," taken by George himself over the Nevada flats during our above-ground atomic testing (now outlawed), has appeared as a symbol of "alien visitors" on more book covers than almost any other type of disk.

Are *they* the "aliens," or do *we* have aliens running our governments all over the world? If *they* (the so-called aliens) have been monitoring us for 40 centuries or more, they are more aware than we are that *Now is the Time* for the ancient truths to be made known. This awareness may include the dangers of atomic energy, when there is plenty of *free energy* available. This "free energy" frightens the Military-Industrial-Religious-Obligarchy (MIRO) to death lest their "orthodox" hold on the *people* may have to be abandoned!

"Orthodoxy" (or the Establishment) and "Intuitive Knowledge" (Gnosticism, Essene-ism, or metaphysics) are opposed to each other in fields other than religion! Is this the answer for those who so often ask, "Why doesn't the government tell us the truth about the UFOs? What are they afraid of?"

Tertullian protested "equal access, equal participation, and equal claims to knowledge" of these "heretics." He especially condemned "the participation of women among the heretics."

I remember that "women's suffrage" came in while I was a young man (for my own mother could not vote until after I was born). But may I remind again that the "Women's Movement" (*Not* just ERA) has become stronger *since* the advent of the saucers (1947). So has the growth of influence among many other minorities.

In light of the difference between "Orthodoxy" and "Gnosticism" of those early centuries, it should become obvious that the same battles between *those in authority* and *the people* (whom those in authority do not always represent) has become more and more critical since World War II (or 1947)!

The change in *awareness* about clean air, clean water, clean land, and many other "New Age Concepts" has already been mentioned in earlier chapters.

The condemnation of "heresy" (the breaking out from the "norm") by "orthodoxy" (the "Establishment") today seems just as fierce as in the realm of religion in the Roman Empire of Nero's day. The buying up of patents that could "free" us, the stigma attached to anyting psychic that would enlighten us to the Invisible Realms, the hounding of anyone who has had "contact" with UFOnauts or Humanoids — these and a hundred other things show how afraid the "orthodox" are today of letting go of their control over *the People!*

In Biblical language, "the devil goeth about as a raging lion, seeking whom he may devour, seeing that his time is short." Don't you see that we are saying the same thing, *except in different language?*

And can't both sides possibly see that we are still engaged in the same old "name-calling" that has gone on for centuries? As long as we continue to use terms such as "Liberal," Conservative," "Fundamentalist," "Non-Christian," "Right Wing/Left Wing," "Believer/Non-Believer," "Radical/Moderate," "Occult/Born Again" — categorizing *everyone* who "does not believe as I do" as a part of the opposition ("heretics") — we deny the fact that *each person is unique in the sight of God.*

In New Testament classes, every astute seminary student studied the difference between the Gospel of John and the Synoptics (Matthew, Mark, and Luke). John's gospel has an altogether different purpose than the other three. But in my day we never heard of the Nag Hammadi Library or the Dead Sea Scrolls. So we did not get the advantage of studying these excerpts from Gnostic and Essene literature. I have discussed Dr. Elaine Pagel's book, *The Gnostic Gospels,* in some detail. It was written in a language a little more understandable than her former book, though both have theological concepts that are rather deep to understand easily.

Her *Johannine Gospel in Gnostic Exegesis: Heracleon's Commentary on John* (copyrighted in 1973) has so many Greek words and complicated theological concepts that I do not want to belabor the reader with a thorough discussion of the work. But for the person who really wants to study the Gnostic interpretation of life and salvation, you can find plenty to ponder in this work. ("Metaphysics" is not something new to Christianity!)

I tried to find this and the *Nag Hammadi Library* by James M. Robinson in several libraries, and I had to wait to send away to a university library for it. About this compilation the cover states: "For the first time in one volume: one of the most dramatic archaeological finds of the century, all the documents of the secret Gnostic writings of ancient Egypt unearthed at Nag Hammadi." The Table of Tractates lists over 60 of these excerpts from many different sources. The jar containing them had been hidden away for a millenium and a half before their re-discovery in the 1940's!

About *The Johannine Gospel in Gnostic Exegesis,* let me put it this way: The Gnostics did not all agree. The Orthodox did not all agree. Each group thought the other group was altogether wrong, but neither group was unanimous in their own opinions within their own group! That is why church councils had to be called time after time — to get some unanimity that could be called "orthodox," and that could claim some "authority" for its adherents. The Gnostics, on the other hand, felt that "if you *know,* you *know*; there is not need to have priests and bishops to tell us what is correct." The "knowing" comes in a way that cannot be explained anyway! And from the other point of view I quote a passage from *The Johannine Gospel:*

> *"Some apologists for the mainstream position as Irenaeus, Hippolytus, Clement, and Origen clearly have little interest in examining gnostic exegesis on its own terms. They denounce it as 'arbitrary,' and 'contrived,' or 'irrational' — accusations certainly appropriate for their polemical intention. Their assessment, however, has too often*

been adopted and repeated by students of early Christian history. (sic!) When Valentinian exegesis is investigated in terms of its own theological principles, however, the diverse fragments of exegesis, even the apparently contradictory interpretations of the same verse, can be seen to derive from a consistent theological structure."

As I read the "Gnostic" interpretations, the "Orthodox" interpretations, and the castigations of each against the others, it reminds me a great deal of my 22-plus years of formal education where one philosopher would point out all the flaws of former ones, and likewise have his own flaws pointed out by the next one to come along. Psychologists like Freud, Jung, and those coming after, did the same thing. And each theologian has his own viewpoint and points out the faults of other theologians. Historians do the same; and indeed, so do scientists! See how long it took "orthodox churchmen" to accept the Copernican system of a "sun-centered universe" instead of "earth-centered!"

So these early battles of thought were no different than many others since that time. It seems to be one of our finite human foibles. As I said before, *Truth is bigger than any person or than any group of persons!*

I have no doubt that there will be plenty of people who will point out many flaws in *this* book. But if it makes a few people think for themselves, instead of parroting something they heard in their childhood, or even from "orthodox" ministers and professors, it will have been worthwhile to spend all this time writing down the concepts that have come out of my own orientation.

The Gnostics seem to have believed there were three different levels of interpretation:

"Heracleon, following Valentinian tradition, applies the metaphysical principle of the three ontological levels of being hermeneutically, discerning in the gospel three distinct levels of exegesis. VISIBLE, HISTORICAL EVENTS perceived through the senses occur at the HYLIC level; the ETHICAL INTERPRETATION of these events is perceived only at the PNEUMATIC level. Whoever understands the text PNEUMATICALLY, then, transcends the mere HISTORICAL level, and transcends as well its ETHICAL meaning. He comes to interpret the whole SYMBOLIC-ALLY." (Emphases mine — Author)

Dr. Pagels then proceeds to spend much of the rest of the book showing the difference in the gospel of John between these three levels of interpretation. And under the chapter "Two Types of Conversion," she has 1) The "centurion's son": an image of psychic salvation, and 2) The "Samaritan woman": an image of pneumatic redemption, interpreted, from the gnostic viewpoint *symbolically*. All the people mentioned in these two stories are also *symbolic* of a *higher truth*.

It reminds me of the *Metaphysical Bible Dictionary* of the Unity School of Christianity (1953, first published in 1931) where, in addition to the ordinary meaning of the Biblical words, a metaphysical interpretation of important words is given in great detail, with the obvious intent of "raising the Christ-consciousness" of the reader.

CHAPTER 11

Orthodoxy Versus Gnosticism In The Early Church

1. THE NATURE OF GOD. Marcion, a Christian from Asia Minor, was struck by what he saw as the contrast between the creator-God of the Old Testament, who demands justice and punishes every violation of his law, and the Father whom Jesus proclaims — the New Testament God of forgiveness and love. He concluded that these must be two different Gods. The majority of Christians condemned this view as dualistic, and identified themselves as orthodox by confessing one God, who is both "Father Almighty" and "Maker of heaven and earth."

Various of the Nag Hammadi texts quoted by Dr. Pagels talk about the creator's arrogance as he says, "There is no other god apart from me"; whereas Faith saw this as impiety of the "chief-ruler" and reprimanded him, stating that 'an enlightened, immortal humanity (anthropos) exists before you!"

Christians today, ignorant of the immensities of space, have been heard to ask, "Can heaven be big enough for all the people that have ever lived on earth?" They are usually the ones also ignorant of the possibility of reincarnation on other planets, surrounding other stars (suns), which themselves orbit in other galaxies! Could it be that the creator-God could be the God of this planet, the Solar Logos of all the planets that orbit *our* sun; whereas Jesus Christ came from the Lord of all universes or galaxies? (Even the term "Universe" means different things to different people, depending upon the mind that comprehends our "little universe of planets" or "*all* the planetary systems, galaxies, black holes, quasars, and systems beyond our ken!) Are the "visitors from Outer Space" like us (some are) or completely different (others are)? Could they enlighten us on this Gnostic idea?

Another of the Nag Hammadi Library texts, *The Secret Book of John,* has this section:

> In his madness he said, "I am God, and there is no other God beside me," for he is ignorant of the place from which he had come . . . And when he saw the creation which surrounds him and the multitude of angels around him which had come forth from him, he said to them, "I am a jealous God, and there is no other God beside me." But by announcing this he indicated to the angels that another God does exist; for *if there were no other one, of whom would he be jealous?* (emphasis added).

2. THE STATUS OF WOMEN.
IS "GOD" MALE, OR FEMALE, OR BOTH?

Many of the deities of the ancient Near East were one or the other, but having a counterpart. One was male, his consort female. But the God of the Hebrews was definitely male, according to the masculine epithets we find in the Bible, such as king, lord, master, judge, and father. "HE is my God" (Exodus 15:2 and elsewhere).

Here is a paragraph from Dr. Elaine Pagel's book *The Gnostic Gospels:*

> One group of gnostic sources claims to have received a secret tradition from Jesus through James and through Mary Magdalene. Members of this group prayed to both the divine Father and Mother: "From Thee, Father, and through Thee, Mother, the two immortal names, Parents of the divine being, and thou, dweller in heaven, humanity, of the mighty name . . ." Other texts indicate that their authors had wondered to whom a single, masculine God proposed, "let US make man (Adam) in our image, after our likeness" (Genesis 1:26). Since the Genesis account goes on to say that humanity was created 'male and female' (1:27) [Androgynous?], some concluded that the God in whose image we are made must also be both masculine and feminine — both Father and Mother.

Notice that the Roman Catholic Church still uses the term "Mother of God," but they have substituted Mary in place of the gnostic idea of the creator-God having a mother. Their term refers to the Mother of Jesus. Many metaphysical groups pray to "Father-Mother God," realizing that at least in the corporeal world there is polarity in all things! And *balance* must be the rule in realms of spirit!

Note how the religious attitudes of a male God in Judaism, Christianity, and Islam were carried over into the social fabric of society. Women veil themselves, dare not "speak in the church," are not considered "the head of the house"; and in many other variations this male supremacy has carried over into modern day culture. Not too long ago female writers used male names in order to be accepted (e.g., "George" Elliott, etc.).

Very recently this has changed, although women are still "fighting for their rights" (equal pay for equal work, the one we hear about the most). The more orthodox churches still hold out against ordination of female priests and ministers. Many that are more liberal are now allowing this too; and many churches would have gone under financially and spiritually if it had not been for "the women's work!"

Dr. Elaine Pagels (note the sex!) reminds us of the contemporary social crises concerning sexual roles, adding that "The Nag Hammadi sources challenge us to reinterpret history — and to re-evaluate the present situation."

The Nag Hammadi Library is replete with references to the equality of the sexes. They could teach, baptize, offer the eucharist, take priestly functions, enact exorcisms and undertake cures; whereas orthodoxy prohibited *all*. By the late second century, the orthodox community came to accept the domination of men over women as the divinely ordained order, not only for social and family life, but also for the Christian churches.

Are we starting all over in this battle? Is it pure coincidence that all of the following are in the same century — the social crises over the equality of sexes, of clergy and laity, of minorities, of *the people* and the rulers — and the finding of the Dead Sea Scrolls, the Nag Hammadi Library, and the contact with *higher beings* all over the planet?

2. THE NATURE OF JESUS

Gnostics and Orthodox disagreed on this point also, and *both* held that their view gave them superior authority.

The Orthodox held to the literal, bodily resurrection of Jesus. This bears enormous implications for the *political structure* of the community. "First, it restricts the circle of leadership to a small band of persons whose members stand in a position of in-contestable authority. Second, it suggests that only the apostles had a right to ordain future leaders as their successors." (Pagels) By using the appropriate gospel passages, Peter was said to be the first to see the risen Jesus. He becomes the only one who can appoint successors. (They seemed to ignore other passages that said Mary Magdalene was the *first* to see the risen Savior. After all, she was a woman!)

The Gnostics, however, claimed their authority from the visions of the risen Jesus which they had had. And if Jesus told them certain things in their ecstatic visions, who were the bishops or clergy to tell them anything that they (the bishops) had *not* experienced? Gnostics had their authority "from Jesus," not from "mere mortals" called clergy! And so the battle continued for authority.

The same thing is happening again today! The clergy who have "graduated from an accredited seminary" take little stock in the fact that certain spiritual persons *do have authentic visions today!* After all, they did not read about this in their seminary training, except perhaps in the history of Joan of Arc. Or in their psychology courses — where "those who have visions" are usually studied from the standpoint of some delusion or hallucination of an errant mind.

Of course, there are such things as "delusions of grandeur," and it is sometimes difficult to distinguish between the two. But "unauthentic" delusions do not disprove (or "dis-authenticate") true visions of people who are so "spiritual" that their "golden auras" can be seen by clairvoyants. This is their "authentication!"

Today there are also those with a certain amount of psychic or spiritual ability, but far from perfect, who suddenly come out with an attitude of authority which seems to imply that they have no use for the Church, because their knowledge (gnosis) is far superior to what they would receive in the Church. And their followers do what the leader does, and *they* forsake the influence they might get from the church, and the influence they might have *upon* the Church!

Don't forget that I have been in *both places,* and I still see a tremendous place for the Church! As I stated before, there are those in the church who have no interest in anything further than "blind faith," and will not reach out further. *Who is to minister to them and their needs?* The Church *must be there to do so!*

But there are plenty of Church-goers who *hunger and thirst* for something more than what the seminaries teach. But they still believe in the mission of the Church to reach out into the world with the grand message of salvation. If ministers can make oblique references to things metaphysical, those people will often come to the minister privately (as Nicodemus did to Jesus at night) and ask what was meant by "that certain remark you made."

Few are the people that will not sit up and take notice if the minister says about the scene on the Mount of Transfiguration: "I wonder what the two men who had been dead for hundreds of years said to Jesus on that mount. I wonder how Jesus knew who they were. I wonder how Peter, James and John knew who they were."

You see, we have used the phrase "The Transfiguration Experience" so often that our minds see only the "glistening garments of Jesus," and forget what *the rest of the story* was. The minister would not need to go so far as to call it the "Hilltop Séance" (which might get him in trouble). But if he even makes the oblique reference stated above, he had better be ready with the proper answer if a parishioner should inquire!

Without going into too much detail about the gnostic interpretations about the passion and death of Jesus, I do want to quote some of the passages, some of which survived orthodox denunciations and were around even before the Nag Hammadi find. It sounds much like the stories one reads in publications about the "Masters of the Far East" today, who "appear" and "disappear" in a moment of time, sometimes remaining just long enough to give a certain person an important message for him/her and his/her mission, and then leave as quickly and mysteriously as they came. It has amazed me that three times in my ministry I have met people to whom the Master Djwal Khul has appeared and who speaks with them telepathically later, after his "appearance." In each case, these three persons have a mission to perform and go on their way, quietly accomplishing that mission. Those are experiences no one can control — not the religious "orthodoxy," not the political tyrants, *no one!* These are people the authorities know nothing about. The ones so contacted never mention it unless there is a specific spiritual reason that would be helpful to the *one* person to whom they give the message. It is *never* done for publicity! I have known a few people to whom the F.B.I. come for information when they know these psychic individuals might have a vision of something that might happen to the President. This the authorities would probably deny, if one asked them outright. The point is: *We do have spiritual supervision on important matters!*

These "Masters" have the ability to "appear" in different forms, depending on the necessity of the moment. I have a huge picture, created by a psychic, of my deceased grandfather, which did not look like his 1935 appearance at all. But in contacting my grandfather, who is in spirit, I asked about it.

He laughed and said, "I just wanted to appear as I had when you knew me in our Biblical lifetime, to see if you would recognize it."

I had. For when the psychic asked, in the group, "Whose picture is this?" I immediately knew it was mine to take home. Others agreed.

With this in mind, consider one of the most famous gnostic texts — *The Acts of John,* and some quotations from Dr. Pagel's book. The manuscript explains that Jesus was a *spiritual being who adapted himself to human perception.*

We remember several times when "he escaped out of their midst, because His hour had not yet come." Once was in Nazareth, when they tried to throw Him down the village cliff; another time was in Jerusalem. No one "took" Jesus' life: He "gave" it, when the time was right. Now to *The Acts of John,* which tells how James once saw Jesus standing on the shore in the form of a child, but when he pointed him out to John,

> *I (John) said, "Which child?" And he answered me, "The one who is beckoning to us." And I said, "This is because of the long watch we have kept at sea. You are not seeing straight, brother James. Do you not see the man standing there who is handsome, fair and cheerful looking?" But he said to me, "I do not see that man, my brother."*

Going ashore to investigate, they became even more confused. According to John,

> *He appeared to me again as rather bald-headed but with*
> *a thick flowing beard, but to James as a young man whose*
> *beard was just beginning . . . I tried to see him as he was . . .*
> *But he sometimes appeared to me as a small man with no*
> *good looks, and then again as looking up to heaven.*

John continues:

> *I will tell you another glory, brethren; sometimes when I*
> *meant to touch him I encountered a material, solid body;*
> *but at other times again when I felt him, his substance was*
> *immaterial and incorporeal . . . as if it did not exist at all.*

John adds that he checked carefully for footprints, but Jesus
never left any — nor did he ever blink his eyes. All of this demonstrated to John that his nature was spiritual, not human. It
sounds to me like humans in their ascended state, with "master-
ful abilities!"

These references remind me of the many times when "Masters" or UFO occupants (are they synonymous?) were seen and
spoken with in homes or restaurants, and when they walked out
the door, were instantly invisible, even though friends, who
wanted one more word with them, had gone immediately to the
door, only to find no one in the street or on the sidewalk.

And there was the instance at a Spiritual Frontiers Fellowship Conference, the first one at which we had a speaker on
UFO's, when the man across the congregation (the one with the
dark glasses) had suddenly left an empty seat when I went
around the congregation to speak to him. I had watched, to be
sure he didn't also leave before the group was dismissed. But
when I got around to that side, the seat was empty. Either he
disappeared, or else that empty seat had had only an "appearance to me" of someone with dark glasses being in that seat!
Those are the two only possibilities.

Did the Master, Jesus, have similar abilities even before the
Resurrection?

He surely did *after* the Resurrection, for the two disciples, on
Resurrection morning, walked with him on the road to
Emmaus, talking about Jesus, and having him quote Scriptures about himself to them — *without their recognizing Him at*
all! Only when He performed a familiar act, breaking and blessing of the bread at their meal, did they recognize him. Then he
disappeared!

4. THE QUESTION OF AUTHORITY. WHY DID ORTHO-
DOXY WIN?

Several things must be considered to answer this question. The Gnostic idea of the Nature of God (dualism?) was one. It could be confusing to the "non-gnostic" (those who had not had the "gnostic experience") to consider a "creator-God" and another Being higher than He!

The Nature of Christ was another reason. Only a "Gnostic" could understand Christ "above the sufferings" of Jesus on the cross, and not be affected by them. Consequently, the human suffering of Jesus gave impetus to the later martyrdoms; if Jesus suffered so, who am I to refuse to suffer for him? And the martyrs, who took suffering willingly, changed the onlookers into believers: "If they are willing to suffer for their beliefs, they must have something I don't have." And they would seek further to find the answers.

So it was the suffering that finally was responsible for the well-known saying, "The blood of the martyrs has become the seed of the Church." As Pagels says: "I suggest that persecution gave impetus to the formation of the organized church structure that developed by the end of the second century."

And Gnostic experiences took many forms, and were often individualistic rather than similar. One would "come to know" or "have a vision" different from that of another Gnostic. Each one *knew*, but his personal experience was his own, not someone else's. So there was not the uniformity that developed among orthodoxy which insisted on one's acceptance of the authority of the priest and the bishop. Pagels says:

"We can see, then, how conflicts arose in the formation of Christianity between 1) those restless, inquiring people who marked out a solitary path of self-discovery and 2) the institutional framework that gave to the great majority of people religious sanction and ethical direction for their daily lives. Adapting for its own purposes the model of Roman political and military organization, and gaining, in the fourth century, imperial support, orthodox Christianity grew increasingly stable and enduring."

Pagels, in her conclusion, suggests that there are fundamental questions that are reopened by the discoveries at Nag Hammadi.

They suggest that Christianity might have developed in very different directions — or that Christianity as we know it might not have survived at all. Had Christianity remained multiform, it might well have disappeared from history, along with dozens of rival religious cults of antiquity. I believe that we owe the survival of Christian tradition to the organizational and theological structure that the emerging church developed. Anyone as powerfully attracted to Christianity as I am will regard that as a major achievement.

We all know, if we give it a little thought, that it is the winners in any conflict — political, military or religious — who write the history — *their way.* (Wouldn't it be wonderful to have the whole history of this planet re-written by the Guardians from Space who have had no axe to grind, except the progress of *Homo sapiens?*)

Pagels continues:

No wonder, then, that the viewpoint of the successful majority has dominated all traditional accounts of the origin of Christianity. Ecclesiastical Christians first defined the terms (naming themselves "orthodox" and their opponents "heretics"); then they proceeded to demonstrate — at least to their own satisfaction — that their triumph was historically inevitable, or, in religious terms, "guided by the Holy Spirit."

If Pagels is right in her assumption from all her studies of the "Gnostic Gospels" that Christianity as we know it might not have survived at all if it had not been for the "orthodox structure" that grew into the Church that the ordinary person could accept, then modern-day "metaphysicians" have something to consider before "throwing out the baby with the bath water!" *The Church does have its place!*

The Church today is divided, and has many faults. But it is not any more divided, nor does it have any more faults, than modern metaphysicians. Anyone acquainted with "Psychic City — Phoenix" can see that even in the Omega New Age Directory (which surely does not include *all* metaphysically-minded persons), there are a hundred or more groups or churches. Why aren't all metaphysicians in *one group?* For the same reason there are hundreds of Christian churches, besides the cults that are not a "denomination" — *Truth is too big for any one person or any one group to be able to express it all!*

So each "modern gnostic" presents the truth as he sees it, just as each denomination presents the "Truth of the Bible" as each sees it. One stresses one form of government differently than another. But, however limited the modern church is, *They do have a program for the world,* not just for each individual who "has a vision or a spiritual gift!" In the church, as in metaphysics, we need to see that we are *not competitors* but *cooperators,* and each group can learn something from other groups. The Church has an interdenominational council, metaphysicians have "psychic fairs," where each can learn from the other!

We need metaphysicians, for they have truth to offer that is not found in most churches. But there are many "hungry Christians" in the church that would seek out a metaphysician, *if he/ she were in the Church!* There is *fellowship of kindred minds* in the Church. Individual students of metaphysics also need *fellowship,* so they don't feel that they are the only ones who think or believe or study this type of thing. If Church Christians could only understand a little metaphysics, maybe leaders in the realm of metaphysics would find their place in the Church!

The original purpose of this book was to show church people that their religion started with metaphysical principles, which got lost somewhere along the way; and to show students of metaphysics that they belong in the church to show the way to progressively-minded seekers of truth.

CHAPTER 12

The Origin of Man
Upon The Earth

I N THE SUMMER of 1925 William Jennings Bryan and Clarence Darrow fought one of the great legal battles of history, sometimes called "The Trial of the Century." John T. Scopes, a 24-year-old biology teacher, was on trial for teaching Darwinian evolution in the public schools of Tennessee, which was prohibited by state law. The question in 1925 was: Should the scientific evidences for evolution be taught to public school children along with the evidences for creation?

Nearly sixty years later the battle rages again, but this time it is called "Scopes II" or "Scopes I in Reverse." The question now is: Should the scientific evidences for creation be given equal time with those evidences for evolution?

State Senator Bill Keith, a member of the Louisiana Legislature, has written a book called *Scopes II — The Great Debate,* in which he discusses this issue. In his prologue he makes this statement:

> *Some historians believe he (Scopes) was recruited by Roger Baldwin, the founding father of the American Civil Liberties Union, just to test the Tennessee law governing evolution. Baldwin did hand-pick Darrow to defend Scopes.*
>
> *Darrow, who performed with great skill, said during the trial that teaching only one theory of origins is sheer bigotry. He also asked the question: "Can the human mind be limited by law in its inquiry after truth?" His question parallels the question creation scientists are asking today.*

The Seventh Day Adventists in their church periodicals have

been spending a lot of time trying to show the fallacies of geological interpretations of millions of years of earth time. They have shown how in Iceland, for instance, in fifty years' time after volcanic eruptions, the same evidence shows there as geologists use to claim millions of years between sedimentary deposits elsewhere. Others have also joined what could be interpreted as "creation science."

My point here is not to debate these conflicting (or supplementary?) theories. Rather I would like to repeat Clarence Darrow's statement and question in the light of today's information coming through dozens of "channels" throughout the world.

That statement and question is: "Teaching only one theory of origins is sheer bigotry. Can the human mind be limited in its inquiry after truth?"

As additional evidence, which will add fuel to the fire of inquiry if ever taken seriously, let me quote from "Matton," channeled through Thelma Terrill ("Tuella"). He was given this appointment by Kuthumi (one of the Three Wise Men recorded in Matthew chapter 2, now an "Ascended Master"). Matton speaks as a representative of all of the Alliance and the entire Space Confederation: (My point is quoted within the following con text, and is *CAPITALIZED BY ME.* — Author)

We of the Volunteer Space Program to the planet Earth have coordinated every effort and all our energies toward these days. We have longed and dreamed to see that hour when Earth should qualify to become a member of its own Solar System. At long last that moment is about to come to pass, when Earth will voluntarily enter the Galactic Pact, and willingly assume the treaties and rules and that great document of Universal Peace. Earth must be willing to honor that commandment which states, "Thou shalt not kill," whether by war or any other cause. Then shall there be peace throught the firmament of the Heavenly Father. WE MUST ASSUME SOME OF THE RESPONSIBIL- ITY FOR THE ACTS OF YOUR PLANET, FOR IT WAS TO YOU THAT WE SENT THOSE DISRUPTIVE AND REBELLIOUS UNITS OF CONSCIOUSNESS WHEN OUR HEAVENS WERE CLEANSED OF ALL WAR- LIKE PROPENSITIES. AS THE CLEANSING TOOK PLACE ELSEWHERE, YOUR PLANET BECAME THE RECIPIENT OF THOSE UNWORTHY ONES WHO

WERE LEFT TO MINGLE WITH YOU, AND TO
PROPAGATE WITHIN YOUR SOCIETY. (Tuella adds:
"The fugitives of Maldek." I would add: "The Lucifer-
ians.")

We have all, therefore, joined our forces and offered our
time and technology to finally rescue the beautiful planet
of Earth from the hold of these malevolent forces of
Lucifer, that rely upon death and destruction and bondage
of humanity. That . . . bondage shall be broken, for all men
must be free! They must be loosed to follow the dictates of
their own inner guidance and inner divine convictions for
their lives and their world. Thus it has been that the wheat
and the tares have been allowed to grow together, but now
that harvest has come.

We of the Universal Confederation, Guardians of your
planet, are the reaping Angels who shall come to separate
the chaff and to gather the wheat into the Father's store-
house. We of other worlds accepted this responsibility to
your planet and your people. Our service to the Radiant
One has been long and steadfast and loyal.

Now compare this dictation with what Jesus said about the
wheat and the tares in Matthew 13:24-30, with the interpretation thereof in verses 36 to 43. Of course this was stated as a parable. But when the disciples asked him why he spoke to the general public in parables he said, "To you it has been given to
know the secrets of the kingdom of heaven, but to them it has
not been given . . . I speak to them in parables, because seeing
they do not see, and hearing they do not hear, nor do they
understand. But blessed are your eyes, for they see, and your
ears, for they hear." (Matthew 13:10-17) So will it be with many
today who read these words!

In Matthew 25:31-46 and Luke 9:26 also are references to
Jesus' return *with these Holy Angels!* "He that hath ears to
hear, let him hear!"

Not only was the "bad seed" brought to this planet, as admit-
ted by Matton in the above dictation, but Brad Steiger (and his
wife, Frances) have brought out in their two books *The Star
People* and *The Seed* much evidence that the "good seed" was
also planted here millenia ago. They have produced question-
naires that have gone out to thousands of people all over the
planet who have certain characteristics, physical as well as

mental and emotional, that are different from most of us. These
are "the Seed" that are now being "awakened in their consciousness" to the heritage that is theirs — and to the "mission" they
have in helping these "Holy Angels" in *their* mission of freeing
this planet from its quarantine from the rest of the Solar System
and this and other galaxies.

There is still more to add to the grist for the mill discussing
the origin of man. This comes from another "Message From An
Outer Craft," and through a different channel: "Sari." Phrado,
Mediator for the "instrument" and a space craft cruising just
outside the earth range, gives this as a part of a longer message:

> *Of course we have a base on the planet Moon, but then,*
> *we have a base of operation on every inhabited planet.*
> *This is part of the plan. And now in closing we will let you*
> *in on a secret: We are also present on uninhabited planets*
> *to HELP CELLS AWAKEN FROM THEIR EMBRYONIC*
> *STATE OF CONSCIOUSNESS. THEIR DESIRE TO*
> *EVOLVE (CELLS) ATTRACTS US TO THEM.* (CAPS
> are mine. — Author)

Let both the Darwinian "evolutionists" and the "creation-
scientists," as well as the American Civil Liberties Union, now
think again about Clarence Darrow's statement and question:
"Teaching only one theory of origins is sheer bigotry. Can the
human mind be limited in its inquiry after truth?"

CHAPTER 13

Past Life Visions -
A Christian Exploration

I N TRYING TO tie together modern orthodoxy and metaphysical truth as I have experienced it in 45 years in the
ministry, I found a book that has tried to do the same thing,
in a much different manner. In looking for books on Gnosticism, metaphysics, spiritual healing, reincarnation and other-
worldliness, I found this title intriguing — *Past Life Visions* —
A Christian Exploration. It is a fairly new book (1983) and is
what it claims to be, "a Christian Exploration."

However, William de Arteaga, the author, uses so many letters to stand for experiences that one gets confused, unless he
writes down those letters as he comes to them so he can refer
back to them when finding them later in the book. For Past Life
Visions he uses PLVs. Later he uses EJR for "Elijah-John Relationships" and ACR for "Act-Consequence Relationship" (instead of "Cause-Effect"). To add to the confusion we find CFO
for Camps Farthest Out, started by Glenn Clark; and SFF for
Spiritual Frontiers Fellowship, which I mentioned earlier in
this book. However, when discussing Edgar Cayce he forgot to
call the study of his readings ARE (Association for Research
and Enlightenment).

PLVs, however, are not what one assumes at first — remem-
brances of past lives. He uses the term very broadly and has five
hypotheses that he discusses: namely, "Subconscious Inven-
tion," "Genetic Memory," "Demonic Counterfeit," Empathetic
Identification," and finally "Reincarnation."

He seems to have not only a very good understanding of Catholic, Orthodox, and Protestant theology but an excellent background in metaphysical groups, the occult, mediumship, charis-

matic movements, and healing-prayer and meditation techniques.

He is open to all these various experiences and treats them all fairly, to my way of thinking. He discusses Middle Ages dogma which made the subject of reincarnation anathema (heretical), although some of the early church fathers proclaimed it. He discusses fundamentalists and their dogmatic approaches. He elaborates on spiritualism, which at one time switched from a "no reincarnation" dogma to a "reincarnation stance," and points out the dangers of getting into the demonic with trance mediumship. His "induced PLVs" were never hypnotic or in the trance state, but rather in a mildly suggestible state of consciousness.

His bibliography is enormous, showing him to be a real student of many avenues of thought. Yet, in discussing some healing techniques that may be fairly successful, if they are of a secular nature he points this out, noticing that prayer and a Christian background is not there. The reason for this is again the danger (in hypnosis and several other non-Christian techniques) of demonic influence. Sometimes the person having the PLV experience is convinced of its authenticity because the information is such that "a prophecy comes true" or something to that effect. Then, later, if contact is continued with the "guide," there might be a gradual shift away from Christian attitudes, once the groundwork of authenticity is established. So the word *discernment* comes into his work very early in the book, this being an important gift of the *Holy Spirit*.

> In attempting to sift among the alternate hypotheses about PLVs we need to be aware that two factors have deeply influenced contemporary Christendom. The first is the decline of dogmatism or, more positively put, the acceptance of ambiguity in theology. The second factor is the rise of occult metaphysical and spiritualist groups and the spread of their ideas to the population at large.

The author points out that the Medieval Church believed with great assurance that the earth was the center of the universe, and Galileo's telescope was thought to be an instrument of the devil. The modern scientific spirit has had a positive effect on most Christians in regard to the way they understand religious truths.

ARCHANGEL LORD MICHAEL, mentioned in the Biblical book of Daniel several times; also in the New Testament book of Jude and Revelation, chapter 12.

EL MORYA and KUTHUMI were (in former lifetimes) two of the three Wise Men who "saw His star in the East" and came to worship Jesus, as recorded in Matthew's Gospel, chapter 2. It is reported that KUTHUMI was also known as Pythagoras and St. Francis of Assisi and was the builder of the Taj Mahjal. He is now one of the well-known Ascended Masters of the Far East and is helping in many ways to "raise the consciousness of Mankind" for the coming Aquarian Age. I have no doubt that such entities have inspired me to write parts of this book. I have information from two other Higher Sources that this book should be printed, and it has been called a "Bridge between Church People and metaphysically-minded people."

Hartman Bau (affectionately, "Papa Bau" from my childhood days) who was the Methodist minister of the Gordonville, Missouri church where my father first met my mother, Lillian, during their childhood. "Papa Bau" had many psychic experiences, one of which saved my grandmother's life, while he was minister of that church.

"Papa Bau," who Bernyce had met just after we were married, also visited with her in her dreams, and gave us much sound advice, including the fact that I really **should stay in the ministry,** *which I did! He was trusted in the "Heavenly Library" (Akashic Records?), so when I became so interested in re-embodiment, he actually looked up several of our past lifetimes together (his, mother's, Bernyce's and mine) that had bearing on why I was in the ministry this time — and what my mission was!*

Author Milton H. Nothdurft, minister and Aquarian Age investigator.

In 25-years of teaching, Bernyce Nothdurft often confounded students with her psychic ability to tell when they were lying to her. They often deceived their classmates, but not their teacher. Such an ability has often helped the author to discriminate between the UFO lecturer who was telling the truth and who was faking his information. Bernyce also used her unusual psychic talents to guide the Nothdurft family.

My personal friend, Kenneth Arnold, now deceased. As early as 1949, he showed me incontrovertible proof not only of fantastic disc maneuvers, but of their speeds that were more than twice the speed of sound, a barrier Earth airplanes did not surpass for many years. He was a well-respected businessman in his area of the U.S.

Specifically, Christians are now aware that spiritual growth is more than merely accepting intellectual docrines or creeds, and that maturity of spirit is a multifaceted process . . . The problem for the Christian is essentially that of releasing our rigid dependence on doctrines, while retaining and growing in our faith in God through Jesus and our belief in scripture. Without these last elements no authentic Christian spirituality is possible.

I pointed out before that a study of ancient truth, metaphysics, and many other avenues of thought seemed to come in the "UFO age" beginning in the late 1900's and getting a tremendous acceleration after the atomic age began. Remember, the UFOs were here before electricity, electronics and space travel began; but our dabbling in the dangerous atomic toys, for which we were not ready, brought them in great numbers immediately, ten years before Earth's first satellite circled the globe. These metaphysical concepts, the Dead Sea Scrolls, the Nag Hammadi Library all accelerated our eagerness to know more spiritual truths *Right Now*. De Arteaga points out that:

The wide proliferation of occult and metaphysical ideas of the past decades . . . reached a high point in the mid-1970s, and are currently in subdued postures. Nevertheless these ideas generated much discussion on the nature of man and the cosmos that have been entertained by orthodox Christians for fifteen centuries. The more conservative Christians feel that the best way to confront the issues raised by the occult is to reassert dogma and ignore or suppress occult ideas. This may or may not be effective but, as we shall show, it is neither a mature response nor one that is Biblically warranted. Yet to accept occult or metaphysical ideas or to wholeheartedly embrace very new meditation technique would be to repeat at the opposite extremes the mistakes of the 1960s when academic theologians attempted to accommodate the Gospel message to the world view of "secular man," a perspective that excludes the transdendent.

A way that is different from both the dogmatic negativity of conservative Christians and the gullible acceptance of metaphysical "seekers" is needed. This method of evaluation would demand a form of spiritual wisdom called dis-

cernment, without which mature judgments on spiritual phenomena are simply not possible.

In later chapters then he makes a case for mature, biblical discernment that seems to guard against the demonic, which some people seem to think is in *all* metaphysical concepts.

He has much material, from case studies, about inner healing that took place by means of induced PLVs. He feels that many places in the Third World countries especially, these techniques could be used to heal many of the physical, mental and spiritual problems that exist in these particular parts of the world. By an induced PLV, and regressing the person back to a very young age, Jesus can be brought to that person for healing, even though that person, later in life, might have developed a prejudice against Jesus as Lord.

I remind the reader that this "regression" is *not* in trance, but is done with the full cooperation of the person who needs healing of the body or of the memories. The Lordship of Jesus is never forsaken, and all is done in an atmosphere of Christian prayer. It goes *much* farther than psychiatry, and even farther than most Christian psychologists.

Personally, this fits my philosophy expressed earlier in this book, that whatever unusual experiences I have been led into, my faith is still as strong in the Lord Jesus Christ as that night that I went to the altar with my mother beside me praying for me; only now it is a much more mature understanding of Jesus, of the cosmos and how it operates, of the nature of man (a "trinity" of another kind), and of each person's relationship to the rest of "the Body of Christ" (the Church). I have been "born again" . . . and again . . . and again . . .

De Arteaga's final chapter is on "Testing the Fruit" of the PLV experience, and of the EJR-ACR-based theologies. After all, there are no books on the subject yet. His experiences are always to be tested by "The Body of Christ" (The Church); his is not as dogmatic as Medieval Catholicism or many Protestants who claim their way as *The Way.* He suggests that healing teams, professional and semiprofessional, with experience in inner-healing could begin to use PLVs as part of their Christian service. "Indispensable would be the consistent monitoring of the sensors for both short- and long-range effects."

Still more exciting is the prospect he offers of evangelization by utilizing the EJR-ACR theology. Not only could individual

PLV healing be done, but he suggests it for mass evangelization!

> *Whether preaching with a theology based on the EJR-ACR can be more effective to large numbers than orthodox preaching is something that must be left to testing discernment. Much modern evangelization is based on the method of preaching the sinfulness of man and the consequence of this sin, eternal loss and hellfire. This is a product to a great extent of Augustinian theology, developed among those already exposed to the Gospel. The emphasis is on individual choice and responsibility for accepting the call of the Lord. This is neither wrong nor ineffective . . . Many persons respond dramatically to this sort of evangelization.*
>
> *Yet it is based on an unbalanced interpretation of scripture. The primary meaning of salvation is not to get to heaven and avoid hell, but "to enter the Kingdom of God," and escape the Kingdom of Satan.*

In conformity with the purpose of my book, I find this author asking the same question I would:

> *The Logos made great use of various metaphysical groups for its revelatory tasks . . . New Thought was similarly influential in bringing to attention the positive aspects of the ACR, especially in regard to prosperity and health. The question comes to mind: Why didn't the Logos move among the orthodox churches on these matters? The answer to such a question is complex, but certainly a part of the answer lies in the fact that the orthodox churches were perfectly satisfied with their credal definitions and theological understandings. There simply was no room in the inn for the Logos; he had to settle for a smelly stable to bring forth his new light.*

Strangely, the author mentions "outer space beings" as being a part of the "guides" of mediums in spiritualism, but UFO is not among the initials used as part of his discussion of phenomena. I am surprised, for he is "up" on so many other New Age concepts. And as I said before, UFOs have not been only "lights in the sky" but solid objects on the ground, out of which came

Beings that conveyed knowledge beyond the knowledge of the recipients, even though they looked just like our human beings on earth. But then he also omitted the dictations of "Masters" through "channels" who were standing before an audience of many people, the "channels" not being in trance, but fully cognizant of everything that was going on in the room, including strangers that would walk in after the session had started.

But he has a theology and technique that *should* be further examined by "The Church," and used for healing and evangelization.

CHAPTER 14

Did Protestantism Throw Out The Baby With The Bath Water?

MASS — LEADBEATER'S book *The Liberal Catholic Church* shows paintings of the "invisible" building seen by clairvoyants after mass. The pray-ers ask for help from saints and angels, who then help "build" this higher dimension building, which extends beyond the walls of the physical building (and is more beautiful). People walking out on the sidewalk in front of the building are affected by these vibrations all week long, not just while the mass is going on. But worshipers are advised to attend, for the purpose of helping to "build" this other-dimensional building by praying for the help of other-dimensional beings in doing so. Worshipers may not even be aware that they are doing this — so in Protestantism mass was omitted from worship by those who were not "in the know." In other words, as worship became more formal and less mystical, so did the spiritual results diminish!

HOLY WATER — seems like "hocus-pocus" to the uninitiated. But De La Warr's experiments in Oxford of "blessing" ordinary tap water, and taking Kirlian photography of what happened to it before and after shows definite changes in the "power" in the water. Pictures before and after the blessing of the same drop of water are markedly different! (Since learning that, I "bless" the water with which I baptize people!)

INCENSE — Experiments have been conducted in movie theaters, spraying certain odors into the theater, corresponding to what is being seen on the screen. There is quite a difference in the emotional reaction of the viewer! Those who meditate with incense can testify to its efficacy in the process. Of course, each meditator may have to experiment with different fragrances, for the same fragrance may affect two people differently, depending upon their former associations with that fragrance, in this life or others.

BELLS — Anyone acquainted with Pavlov's early experiments with dogs will remember that they responded to certain signals, either visual or audible. They had been conditioned by always getting food upon seeing or hearing the signal; finally salivating when the signal was given although there might not have been subsequent feeding. We are all emotionally responsive to familiar signals; holy water, incense, bells, genuflecting, the feel of "prayer beads"; or in the Protestant denominations, to the singing of hymns, the reading of the Scripture, the time of prayer, offering, etc.

And so in the more metaphysical aspects: candles, music, the feeling of a Presence, self-hypnosis or suggestion, etc. The "familiar" brings "familiar results," a feeling of awe. And with either the orthodox training or the more metaphysical approach, there is hopefully spiritual growth from year to year.

PAIN and PLEASURE have their place in spiritual growth also. In the orthodox approach, many people need counseling to get through the painful experience, or to praise for the pleasurable ones. From the reincarnational approach, one probably does not see "the good" in the painful experience any more than in the orthodox approach; but one has faith that there "must have been some reason" in either case. But through hypnosis the cause is sometimes found to be in a former life. And often when the cause is seen for what it is, or was, one is freed from being tied to the pain any more in this life. Often the problem is actually solved. But sometimes, in either approach, a certain amount of time must transpire before the subject is willing to accept the true meaning and purpose. It is interesting to note in passing that, while phychics can often help others through their problems, they have to go through their own just like anyone else — for their karmic reasons!

FEELING AND SEEING — A fellow pastor in Iowa told me about a particular communion service in which he was overwhelmed at a certain moment with a feeling of something special taking place right then. Every sensitive pastor has had similar feelings, sometimes deviating from his notes at that moment and saying something he had not planned at all. In the particular case mentioned here, this pastor learned later from some of his congregation who he knew had clairvoyant abili-

ties that at that very moment they had *seen* a "Light" or a
"Light Body" behind him or above him.

I have had the same experience, not expressing it to anyone
until one of my clairvoyant parishioners told me what they
"saw" above or behind me (sometimes beside me). When I checked to see what I was saying at the moment they had this vision,
it turned out to be the exact time in the sermon when I was
saying something I had not planned to say in advance; it simply "came to me on the spur of the moment!"

INTUITION OR HUNCHES — Some say "women have intuition; men have hunches." Be that as it may, psychic knowledge comes in various ways to both sexes — information that
could not have been obtained in any other way at the moment.

To illustrate: For ten of the eighteen years I was in my last
parish, a man who lived in the north end of town, across town
from our church, offered to go to all three hospitals and check
the registers to see if we had any patients in any or all of them.
By his doing this in the morning, and phoning it to the office, I
could more easily plan my afternoon, knowing about how much
I had to do, and knowing who the patients were in advance. On
numerous occasions, having completed seeing all the patients
he had reported, I would have a sudden urge to go to a hospital
where no one had been reported, to find that someone had been
checked in *after* my helper had checked the register that morning! Or sometimes I had gone to all three hospitals, called on all
the patients, and had an urge to go back to the first one, only to
find that someone had checked in there, *after* I had been there.
Or they might have *been* checking in while I was calling on the
others but were not placed on the register until an hour later.

Several times the person I then found would say something
like this: "Oh, Reverend, I have just been praying that you would
come. I need a prayer so badly. Would you pray with me?" The
orthodox person might say: "The Lord answered his/her prayer
by sending you to him/her." The person more metaphysically
inclined might put it this way: "You caught the vibrations of
need that emanated from that person, and being sensitive yourself, you went to see who had sent out the message."

Well, whichever way you put it, it is true that "the Lord sent
me" — whether through "The Holy Spirit," or through the *Holy*
Spirit that is in each of us, if we will but *be aware.* "Stir up the
gift of God which is in thee" (II Timothy 1:6), and dedicate that
gift for God's use instead of for selfish purposes!

"AGITATED" SLEEPLESSNESS, A PSYCHIC AWARE-NESS — More times than I can tell, it has happened that I had such a restless night that I had a hard time explaining it to myself — until the next morning. Some parishioner that was very close to me (close emotional tie) had had a heart attack during the night and was in the hospital — or someone had died during the night, often at about the time I was "awakened!" Sometimes it had happened in that town, and sometimes many miles away, and I was called about it in the morning! When I become more spiritual perhaps I'll even be able to recognize *what* or *who* awakened me, and maybe "hear their message."

SEEING AURAS — Another minister friend of mine told me he had been intrigued by those who could see auras around people. He had earnestly prayed to be able to see auras himself, as he thought it would be so helpful in the ministry. He was given the gift, but it was not the blessing he had expected. He told me of the disappointment he had had on occasions when he could "see" what some "outstanding citizen" in the community, or some "pillar of his church" was *really* like! They were not the pious or righteous persons they pretended to be at all. It was such a disappointment in those cases that he prayed for that "gift" to be removed again, and it was! Sometimes we are better off with the gifts *God* gave us than with the ones we *think* we would want. Anyway, the gifts we now have are the ones we have *earned* through lifetimes of service.

I have been helped in some instances by people in my churches that have been able to see auras, and who would use them to help me when asked to do so. (Of course, one does not tell everyone who this is, because it is sometimes embarrassing to them. People hound them with all kinds of questions, which, if they were honest, they really do not want the answers for!)

The "physical" aura is closest to the body, then a second aura, outside of that one, indicates the mental body or the mental capacity of that person. A third one indicates the spiritual condition of that person. (Notice that I did *not* say "religious").

I had a person sitting next to me when our bishop was speaking one time, and this person indicated that the physical aura indicated that the bishop had heart trouble. As discreetly as I could I inquired, months later, of a district superintendent who was on the cabinet just a year or two before this. He corroborated the fact that the bishop had to watch his heart, and was being treated for it, but that this was not well known. I had a difficult time "explaining" how I knew this! Both the bishop and that district superintendent are now gone, and no one else knows that I made such inquiries.

On occasion I have been concerned that a parishioner with a critical health problem might pass away while I had to be far away at a conference of some kind. I would visit this parishioner and take along this person who could see auras, asking this person to particularly watch for the physical aura, to see whether he or she was likely to die very soon. I found this "aura person" to be quite accurate in telling me either that I didn't need to worry while I was gone, or that the person's aura was just about gone!

In the latter case I would call some other minister and ask him "to stop and see the person on the critical list," and "Would you be able to take the funeral in case I don't get back?" Usually however, I just planned that I would have to leave the conference early. This was particularly helpful in the case where several ministers were traveling together in someone else's car; for when I knew the aura was very weak, I would then drive my own car! (Of course the parishioner, the other local minister, and the families did not know what was in my mind — only the "aura person" and myself, and usually my wife.

Another way this gift was helpful in my ministry was in judging certain "metaphysical kooks" or "Metaphysical Pretenders." It took me much longer to figure out whether they were on the level or not than it did these "aura persons." They could see a sham immediately! And they were sometimes disappointed in me that I did not take their word, after I had asked their opinion. But eventually, I learned that they were almost always right in their *first* impression, and that I was not. Sometimes it took me a year to figure out what the "aura person" had seen right away.

This was helpful in going to meetings of a metaphysical nature. To learn that the speaker we went to hear was either "on the level" or that he/she had a beautiful purple or golden spiritual aura, was helpful in judging the worth of what was said. This field is full of very "gullible" people, who believe anything they hear at a metaphysical meeting. To know what the spiritual condition of the speaker is before he starts to speak, and whether or not he speaks *truth* is very helpful in trying not to be gullible.

Many "Intellectuals" who do not have the advantage of an

"aura-seeing" person think that all people who believe in metaphysical stuff are kooks. In fact, most of them are so proud of their "intellect" that they don't even believe in this "aura prattle." The interesting thing is that these aura persons can *see* that these people have a tremendous *mental* aura but with a very *undeveloped spiritual aura* in many cases.

In the early days of the Saucer Club mentioned elsewhere in this book we discovered two persons who could see auras. So to test them in a mildly scientific manner, we put them both in one end of the room, and in the other end sat a man who could "change his aura" according to what he was thinking! If he was thinking beautiful thoughts his aura was *much* different, and a different color, than if he changed to thinking of something sad or bad.

To our surprise, when the man was thinking beautiful thoughts, both "aura persons" saw the same thing, the same colors. But when his thoughts were other than beautiful, they saw different colors than before, but *each saw the same as the other in this case also.* So the whole Club became "believers" quite early, for they trusted both of the persons, who were *not* collaborating with each other while these experiments were going on. These auras are the *Halos* in traditional paintings of saints and Christ.

SIDE EFFECTS (NEW GIFTS) FROM STUDYING TOGETHER. It is a well-known axiom that Christians find strength in going to church and working together for the common cause of Christ. They encourage each other, and find talents they would not attempt if they tried to "be a Christian in a vacuum." The same is true in the metaphysical field, if the persons meet regularly and learn to have mutual friendship and trust. They develop new talents, too.

One example is a talent that developed in a woman who had been strictly orthodox until starting to come to our Club regularly. At work she began to get intuition about things that inspired confidence in those talents among fellow workers.

One day a worker from another office came into hers and said, "I have an error in my books somewhere. I've gone over it time and again, and can't find where the error is. Do you know where it might be?"

Of course, our friend was startled and said, "What makes you think I would know? I have no idea." Both went back to work. In just a few moments our friend walked back into this other person's working quarters and said, "Why don't you look on page 48. I think that's where your error is."

Concentrating then on that *one* page, she found it in no time at all.

"How did you know where it was?" she asked.

To which our friend replied, "Oh, I don't know. It just came to me that it was on page 48!" This gift has grown with time, and she has intuition about many other things.

One man was encouraged to use a gift that seemed to be developing in him. He could just touch one of us and tell us where we hurt. As this gift developed through constant use, he was able to diagnose certain ailments; but as in most cases of this kind, he has to be careful not to get in trouble with medical authorities for "practicing medicine without a license."

(Now isn't that a queer phrase for the medical profession to use at all? "Practicing medicine without a license," when no medicine is involved at all!) It's actually comical, except for the tragedy of it — that many a qualified diagnostician is not able to use such a psychic gift because of the power of a small clique. Just like in the Church!

An Indian "medicine man" that I know can "see in the body with his fingers," and thereby "knows" where the problem originated. Sometimes the *cause* is not *where the pain is,* and he knows that. So he manipulates with his fingers in the place where the *cause* of the problem is, adding certain plants and herbs to the "prescription" so the healing may continue even after his treatment. The "coagulation" in a certain organ, or the "infection," is released by his "operation" which leaves no scar.

And the number of psychics who help the police solve crimes by "finding the body" of a murdered victim, for instance, is much larger than one imagines. Many medical people, psychiatrists, and police still think of this as "hocus-pocus." And so the ones who do use such means have to be quiet about it. But investigators of the psychic find them (through their own psychic ways) and agree not to disclose their findings. And so the Greater Awareness of humanity in general grows constantly, taking in more and more people, until finally maybe all crime can be eliminated in decades to come, by everyone "knowing" things that can no longer be hidden, as Jesus said so long ago.

Now if only the clergy could be influenced to accept these precepts (the Ancient Wisdom) in greater numbers, then the Counselors of besieged humanity could be of so much greater service, instead of wasting so much time arguing "the lesser points of the law" in Conference sessions (as well as wasting so much of the parishioners' "apportionment money" in the process)!

I have read that in the early days of the church only those with psychic and spiritual "gifts" could be priests. One wasn't a "clergyman" unless he was also a psychic.

This information has been effectively "buried" for centuries, ever since competition of the various Mediterranean bishops ended in Rome's bishop becoming the headquarters of the church.

The political process from then on finally prevailed over those with "spiritual gifts." Just as the American Medical Association finally controlled "alleopathy" and for all practical purposes outlawed "homeopathy," in which my own doctor uncle was an esteemed practitioner.

And just as in Protestantism the "ordination process" for ministers is controlled by a small board in the mainline denominations. And many of those not of the mainline denominations consider all metaphysical principles as being "of the devil," even though they heal the body and help the growth of the soul.

Control, control, control! That's the name of the game, whether in ecclesiastical circles, political circles, or economic circles! When will humanity in general ever come to the True Service Motive, and thereby form the True Brotherhood of Man, and the Kingdom of God on Earth?

Howard B. Rand, LL.B., in his *Study In Revelation* shows very definitely the "historical" interpretation of that book, and shows how and when the beginning of the deterioration of this "control" took place. False ecclesiasticism, evil economics, and therefore political phases of human mis-rule are sure to go, and a "new heaven and a new earth" will be born. And that's what The New Age, The New Order of the Ages, is all about! Here again, The Bible and the metaphysical approach are in conjunction.

LIFE AFTER DEATH - "BELIEF" OR "KNOWLEDGE?" - It has been the main thrust of Christianity that life after death was demonstrated by Jesus' Resurrection from the dead. "If in *this* life only we have hope in Christ, we are of all men most miserable. But now is Christ risen from the dead, *and become the firstfruits of them that slept*" (I Corinthians 15:19, 20).

Many Christians have this hope *as a part of their belief*. But I have had Christians who were active in the church say to me,

"I had faith, through the church, that there was life after death. But it wasn't until I began studying modern *proof* in this Club of ours that it became *real* to me. I no longer *fear* death as I did before, even though my *faith* told me it was so."

Many clairvoyants have "seen" a misty substance rise from the earthly body of a loved one at the time of death. And there are the reports of thousands of subjects who had experienced the "death and return" at the time of accident or surgery. The experiences of those who have "seen death" and returned are so similar in so many ways that this is as "scientific" evidence as many other things are that we call "scientific!"

Having met and talked at length with several people who have had the "death experience," I have seen for myself that they do not fear death at all, but rather look forward to it. In most cases they hated to come back, but were told by some "Light Being" that it was not their time; they had more work to do here first. Which is a great argument against suicide as a way to "get there quicker."

Another argument against suicide is reincarnation. Suicide is not "the way out" of any problem, and simply forces everyone else with whom that person had karma to come back again, making all the arrangements on the Other Side to come in together with all those people again, and simply *postpone* the problem that has to be resolved! Too bad we are not taught these things, along with all other spiritual truths, *early in life!* Perhaps it would deter the growing number of teen-age suicides in our society.

ASTROLOGY — BIBLICAL AND MODERN — It is a common practice of some schools of thought to lump astrology and many other spiritual things with the "necromancy" mentioned in Deuteronomy 18:9-14, making no distinction between the things mentioned there and *the use made of these things by the surrounding nations,* which was an "abomination" for the people of Israel who were to trust in their God!

These Christians haven't studied the rest of the Scriptures very carefully, or they would see countless references in Old and New Testaments to the signs of the zodiac!

In Revelation 4:7 John sees four beasts: LION (Leo); A CALF (Taurus); A MAN (Aquarius); and A FLYING EAGLE (Scorpio; according to the old astrology it was called the eagle). These are the four cardinal points in the zodiac, each one had two others between it and the next. This is the same order in which the twelve tribes were encamped around the tabernacle. In Numbers 2 is given the order in which they were to pitch their camps. The "standards" mentioned were similar to what we today would call "flags," each representing some specific distinctive quality. THE LION was the standard of Judah, who was to camp on the EAST. Issachar and Zebulun were the two others on the east. THE MAN was the standard of Reuben, who was to camp on the SOUTH, along with Simeon and Gad. THE BULL was the standard of Ephraim, who was to camp on the WEST, along with Manasseh and Benjamin. THE EAGLE (or Scorpio) was the standard of Dan, who was to camp on the north, along with Asher and Naphtali. I have been informed where (in the United States) these "standards" or "ensigns" are to be found, but that they probably will not be found until near the end of this century — *after the national awakening of this people of "Israel" as to their true identity and destiny!*

In Ezekiel (chapter 1:10 and chapter 10:14) we see again these same astrological signs: A MAN (Aquarius); A LION (Leo); AN OX (Taurus); and AN EAGLE (now Scorpio). The Four Gospels, Matthew, Mark, Luke and John have often been delineated by these same four characteristics, a Lion, an Ox, an Eagle and a Man. There are other references, but these are enough to show that the Bible is full of astrological references. THE WISE MEN, according to the accurate translation of *The New English Bible,* are called "astrologers," and they came to Judea because of a "star which they had seen in the East" pointing to a great personage who was to be born in Judea. They did not know *where* in Judea, and went to the king, who went to the prophets, to find out. Still it is interesting that it was the *star* that directed them in the long journey across the deserts to come *to Judea!*

The difficulty is in *the Use* made of astrology. "Astrologers" who write columns in the papers are as unreliable as the many false predictions of psychics! I have learned from a number of sources that modern astrology is a far cry from the original astrology as known by the ancients. Also, *Spiritual Astrology* is quite different from the astrology practiced by many today. Perhaps the ones who seem so accurate, as opposed to those who make so many errors, is indicative that they *are* using astrology according to the ancient knowledge rather than its modern counterpart.

When people are so "tied to the stars" that they do not make a move without consulting their astrologer, instead of trusting God the Loving Father to guide them according to their own God-given Christ consciousness, this indeed is "an abomination unto the Lord." But at least let us not condemn *all* astrology, and lump it with "necromancy," when the Bible is so full of it. We merely demonstrate our own ignorance when we make such all-inclusive statements!

DREAMS AS A HELPFUL GUIDE — Joseph, son of Jacob, was "a dreamer." In fact, several of his dreams as a youth made his brothers so jealous that they sold him into slavery! But his interpretation of the Pharaoh's dream saved Egypt — and his father and brothers — from starvation. It is a fascinating story in Genesis 37 through 47. Nebuchadnezzar's and Daniel's dreams, and their importance to the future history of the world, are related in the book of Daniel.

The baby Jesus was saved from extinction by Herod, when the "astrologers" (Wise Men in many ways) had a dream that they should not return to Herod but returned to their own country by another way.

Joseph, husband of Mary, the child's mother, had a dream which caused him to flee from Herod's henchmen and find safety for the Holy Family in Egypt. When Herod was dead, Joseph had another dream (while in Egypt) that is was safe to return now — and went to the insignificant town of Nazareth, where Jesus was safe again until the time his ministry should begin in Judea, Samaria and Galilee.

There are many other references in the Bible to significant dreams. This is the way in which the subconscious speaks to the conscious. Modern psychology has studied this phenomena and discovered that dreams are necessary for our sanity! Studies in REM (Rapid Eye Movements) show that when a person has these movements, he is usually dreaming. When regularly awakened during this time, the dreamer can recall the dream. But if the process of awakening him is continued too long, his emotional balance is disturbed. In other words, *Dreaming is necessary for emotional stability,* whether one remembers the dream or not.

Edgar Cayce spoke a great deal about dreams. The Association for Research and Enlightment in Virginia Beach has thousands of accounts on record, and some of their researchers are quite efficient in interpreting dreams. We have discovered that dreams are usually symbolic, as are dreams and visions in the

Bible, and one has to learn what the symbolism means. Dream books are not always accurate, according to these researchers, for the simple reason that certain symbols may mean different things to different people. One has to learn, for instance, what a "symbol of authority" means to *that particular dreamer*. That symbol may be a strict father, a policeman, a military commander, or the bully down the street, depending on the former experiences of *that dreamer*. And his dreams must be interpreted in terms of what that "authority figure" means to him — whether *fear*, or *awe*, or *respect*, or maybe *protection*.

Again, this New Age information fits in with traditional acceptance of dreams as God's way of protecting his people from harm from enemies, personal or national. Many a person has escaped disaster on ship, plane or car by a dream or vision of that disaster, or some similar warning. Why *everyone* was not similarly warned about such disaster may relate to their spiritual condition or karmic necessity.

DREAMING A NEW SKILL — In a former lifetime I rode a horse — a "circuit rider" in the Methodist Church. As far as I know, that was the only prior time I have been a minister, though I have been in a similar profession many times, according to the needs of the environment into which I was born. But this time I got to my first churches by "horsepower" of a motorcycle.

I cannot explain the connection between a horse and a motorcycle; but I *can* say that I learned to ride a motorcycle in my sleep! I needed to have a church in order to finance my last year in college. Before I knew how I was going to get to the church that was provided for me, I actually learned in my sleep how to drive a motorcycle! That was all the transportation I could afford from the meager salary I was to get from that church. There was one available in a nearby city. So a college friend and I got ourselves to Cedar Rapids by the help of some friend who was going there, made arrangements for the purchase of a second-hand four-cylinder Henderson, and were about to return to school.

We were both wondering how this first ride of my life would end, but I assured my friend that I "knew how to drive a motorcycle!" Well, I had a few pointers from the dealer, but my inner knowing was really sufficient. The only problem I had was in turning the throttle a little too much at a time, and my friend sitting behind me was suddenly sitting on the street behind me!

It was a sight to behold! After both of us stopped laughing, he got on again, and I turned the throttle, but this time a little more slowly; and off we went down the street and finally onto the highway, getting back to college without further mishap! Over forty years later we still reminisce about this incident when we get together at Annual Conference. I don't remember whether I ever told him *how* I learned to ride a motorcycle!

Some of the best sermons I ever preached (according to the testimony of my own parishioners) were some that I got in the middle of the night. I learned that no matter how clear the "night messages" were, they would be gone by morning if I did not write them down. So I got into the habit of immediately writing just the bare outline of this tremendous idea that I had received in my sleep. Then I could remember the rest when I awakened.

Whether this was given to me by my own "Super-conscious," or by a friend in the Invisible Realms isn't as important to me as the necessity for "giving thanks" that it happened!

I do believe strongly that I have been guided at other times by Invisible Friends.

There would be times when I wondered about "parallel passages" of a Scripture I was thinking about. The only "four gospel harmony of the gospels" that I ever had was given to me by my preacher-grandfather years before he died. I would go to that for some reason, instead of to my "three-gospel harmony" which I studied in seminary. The "four-gospel harmony" has many side references in the margins. Some of those side references would cause me to go to another book to find explanations for them. In so doing, I would find sentences or whole paragraphs by which I was enlightened about the whole theme I was considering. And sometimes this book's message would lead me to look up something in a fourth book, and so on.

Now, if I had not gone in the first place to my grandfather's "four-gospel harmony" that he had given me, I never would have been led to the second, third, and fourth books as a result; for my own "three-gospel harmony" did not have in it the marginal related verses that made me look up all these other references. My grandfather, of course, had been deceased for years at this time, and we have had many instances that happened to us that make us quite sure that he was still helping us in our ministry!

These also were some of my "better" sermons. So the whole

sermons that came out of a dream experience could have come from either this same source, or from my own sub- or super-conscious, or from the combined consciousness of the race — whichever fits into your scheme of psychology or theology.

Of course, this is really no different from the composers, writers of literature, and inventors who have received inspiration for their various works in a similar manner.

Would that more clergy, physicians, lawyers and many laymen would accept the fact that there are ways of *knowing* besides reading, listening to a lecture, or studying in a prescribed course of study. This is not to say that studying is not important, or that scientific methods are not applicable. But many a person has *known* the truth of something, while it took scientists years to prove this same truth to the world. It is sometimes explained as the "left brain" and the "right brain," one of which is logical and reasoning, the other of which is intuitive. Anyway "mystics" have their place in the world, and so do "scientists" — two perspectives of the same phenomena!

Recently two new conferences were started out of one large Conference of the United Methodist Church. These were split at a Jurisdictional Conference, and they were simply known as the Los Angeles Area and the Phoenix Area. A new bishop was elected for the Phoenix Area. Much preparation, apportionments, and many other things preceded the two "organizing conferences."

The organizing conferences were to be held on the same two days, one in Pasadena, the other in Phoenix. Both started with Holy Communion, as Methodist Conferences always have — and at the same hour, led by the two bishops. They were connected by a telephone line.

It was an exhilarating experience for us (and I'm sure for them) to be able to sing the traditional hymn together — "And are we yet alive, and see each other's face . . .?" We could hear them singing and ourselves, too. The organ was in Pasadena, we in Phoenix. The man leading our singing, conducting with his hands, had earphones on so he could be sure we were together.

Afterward the two bishops greeted each other and gave greetings to the other conference, both of whom both congregations could hear. It was one of the marvels of modern science — and quite an emotional as well as spiritual experience.

I could not help remembering something similar in 1956, when

I had gone with William Dudley Pelley (a veteran in this field) to a "materialization meeting" where I actually saw my mother (who had died in 1934) and dozens of other materialized people from Higher Realms, each of whom had messages for someone in the room. One lady's first husband was one of them (her second husband was sitting beside her). There was no jealousy, only a blessing for her that she was so happy.

Then we continued the singing with which we had started. Two of us sat together who were singers — a tenor and a bass. Soon two women *materialized* and sang with us — a soprano and an alto!

Here we were, singing church hymns, hymns about Jesus, just as if we had all been in the flesh and singing a quartet in church! This was another highlight in my spiritual journey.

There was perfect four-part harmony — two singing in the flesh (tenor and bass), and two singing in the "spirit form" (soprano and alto). We had breached the veil that "separates" us, presumably. It reminded me of the harmony that exists "Over There" all the time, something that Jesus knew as He taught us to pray:

"Thy will be done on earth, *as it is in heaven.*"

The two new annual conferences had sung together by means of a telephone wire — something that would have been impossible a century ago. While it was thrilling, there are those to whom it would not be as emotional because they "know all about telephone technology" and "knew it could happen all along." Singing with ethereal people is just as hard for most people to accept or understand as "intercontinental satellite communication and music" would have been a half century ago, but which we now accept as commonplace!

There still is mystery and awe in all of it! Even tape recorders, and certainly video recorders, are amazing, though we have hundreds of them around us every day. *Our consciousness is being raised all the time,* as we go from one marvel to another. We accept these amazing adventures into the New Aquarian Age almost without thinking. "The Kingdom of Heaven is at hand." Reach out and touch it!

CHAPTER 15

Imminent Changes . . . If The World Knew and Believed.

MUCH OF OUR sociological and psychological attitudes, as well as our religious ethic, is based on wrong assumptions.

In the first place, much of our religious teaching is the "Thou shalt nots." Consider the Ten Commandments. Some people think that if they just "keep the Commandments" they'll do O.K. But at least eight of them are negatives — "Thou shalt not . . . this or that."

What *should* I do? "Love the Lord thy God . . . and thy neighbor as thyself," said Jesus, summing up "the law and the prophets."

And what is "the law and the prophets?"

There is but One Law — the law of cause and effect. *The Prophets* were foretelling what would happen if this *law* is broken, or if it is kept. That may be over-simplification; but if you consider everything that has happened, and that is happening, in the world, doesn't that about take it all in?

If one has a *terrible hatred or prejudice* against any race or color or nationality, outside of the saving grace of a conversion experience how would such a person learn the truth about that race, color or nationality *except to be a MEMBER of that group someday?*

A rich person with no sympathy for the poor might have to live in poverty before he develops sympathy! Homophobia might only be cured by someday learning what it is like to be a homosexual. (Maybe many of our homosexuals had homophobia in a past life, although there is another explanation for it.) Or a poverty-stricken individual without knowledge of reincarnation might not be able to see anything good in a rich person, but only suppose him to be evil just because he's rich. (We must not forget that the person who "asked Pilate for the body of Jesus" and then buried it in his own tomb was the rich Joseph of Arimathea — who had tin mines at the time in England!) *Hatred never breeds good,* either for the person hated, or for the person hating! It is a cancer of the soul — and has a terrible effect on the body, too!

Remember where the word *Prejudice* comes from. It means to *Pre-Judge.* One who judges *after he has the facts* is not guilty of *Pre-judice.* That's why Jesus could say "My judgment is just" (John 5:30). But most of us do not have *all* the facts! Therefore, it behooves us to be tolerant of someone different from ourselves.

From the standpoint of what is learned by a clairvoyant going back into the Akashic records and seeing what caused certain problems, we can see excesses in the opposite direction, too. And the world would certainly be different if people in general saw *the implications* of how a wide-spread belief in reincarnation would change our concepts — so long as its acceptance did not bring back the caste system where one could *never* better himself!

Consider a few examples:

A "do-good-er" who knows nothing of reincarnation is often heard to make a thoughtless statement such as: "He couldn't help it that his skin is black." "He couldn't help it that he was born a Jew, or a Catholic, or a Mexican, or to a prostitute." Or we hear "It was just an accident of circumstance that I was lucky enough to be born in the United States." "Why did he have to be born into such a crazy, mixed-up family?" "People who have an infant with Down's Syndrome should have it aborted as soon as possible." "He died on the Titanic: his time had come and *he had to go.*" And a host of others.

Granted, that many birth defects have been caused by our *atmospheric atomic tests.* We knew this in our "Cup and Saucer Club" at the time this was going on, and I preached against the atomic tests at that time. As I said before, I had to quit because I was scaring pregnant mothers in my congregation, without influencing our federal officials in the least! But later it was proven to be true (science is *always* behind metaphysically-acquired knowledge!), and we ceased our *atmospheric* tests, as I also stated before, and gave the reason.

As a general rule people have *chosen* the kind of environment into which they will be born before coming here *because of the particular lessons they will learn from that experience!* Many have been born into *every* race over many centuries. Such people have few prejudices against any race. Some are born into a family of a particular faith for what they can learn, according to the previous knowledge, or lack of it. Some have chosen "craxy, mixed-up families" to be born into because of the *challenge* of seeing what they can do *with* that environment or *for* certain persons in that family. Some are born to prostitutes, or to any "illicit union," because they are so anxious to get into earth experience again that they will accept *any* conditions, *just so they can get here!*

There are millions on the waiting list, waiting to get in on the excitement of earth life in this particular generation. This is the reason there are so many more millions of people here right now than at any previous time in history or pre-history: they want to get in on the excitement *at this time.* This is an *unprecedented time* to be alive, at least in the last 26,000 years! *This* Aquarian Age the whole solar system is in a different area of space than ever before, and the vibrations are different. (Haven't you noticed how different they are? Have you *ever* experienced conditions like those of today?) Some were born black, or Jewish, or American *because of the particular needs of their souls that needed that environment to perfect certain traits they desired!*

Some people cannot understand where four billion people came from when there were only a few thousand just six millenia ago. But we hear of many nowadays who came from other planets. Some volunteered to come here to help us "no matter how many lifetimes it took to do that." Others were recalcitrants from other planets, sent here to learn to get along with each other, when they wouldn't abide by the Universal Laws of the planets from which they came.

This information came from one of the Space Brothers, Matton, channeling through the well-known "Tuella":

> *We must assume some of the responsibility for the acts of your planet, for it was to you that we sent those disruptive and rebellious units of consciousness when our heavens were cleansed of all warlike propensities. As the cleansing took place elsewhere, your planet became the recipient of those unworthy ones who were left to mingle with you, and to propagate within your society.* —(Tuella, P.O. Box 186, Aztec, NM)

While we are on the subject, let us again digress a moment to discuss "life on other planets." Every time the subject comes up, our erudite "scientists" and "astronomers" assure us that all the planets in this solar system are uninhabitable because the conditions on each one would not sustain life. They always refer to "life as we know it" — physcial and mundane. But life is not all *just as they know it!* That's the trouble with our specialization; each science thinks in its own field, and can't seem to broaden their horizons beyond that known field.

That is one of the reasons for this book! We *need* to broaden our horizons to include many fields.

We have *life un-like what they know,* even here on this planet. There is life, with consciousness and memory and thought processes, in a dimension beyond our visual sight and auditory sound — right here, all around us, every moment, day or night! Ask any psychic or sensitive or clairvoyant or clairaudient person. There are either more of them now than ever before — or else it is just becoming more feasible to talk about it than it used to be.

And these "scientists" tell us that life cannot come from *other* solar systems or galaxies because the time consumed in getting here, even at the speed of light, would be so great that it would be impractical. Besides, "Why would a superior race *want* to come to this tiny planet in an insignificant solar system?"

Again they are "out of their field." What about *Love, Concern, Compassion* as good reasons? If they sent their recalcitrants here when they "cleansed the heavens of warlike propensities," why wouldn't they continue to have an interest, if they were as superior morally and spiritually as they *obviously* are technologically?

And as to "getting here from other galaxies," again we are thinking in terms set forth by Albert Einstein when we say "nothing can exceed the speed of light." Though he was brilliant beyond my comprehension, we hear every once in a while of other scientists who seem to know that the great Einstein had other things to tell us that he didn't get told before he left this "life as we know it." Was he about ready to modify his "theory of relativity?"

And what if a *thing* would lose its mass if it exceeded the speed of light? We are living in a whole universe of *energy.* What about the possibility of *teleportation* — dismantling atoms into electrical energy, or energies even travelling faster than electri-

city, and re-assembling them at a distant point? Science fiction?
Yes, science fiction like television, sending pictures from Europe
into space and back again from a satellite to a receiving set
across the ocean — or from the moon to earth. If we have done it
with pictures, why not with *matter?* It's *all* energy!

*Broaden your horizons, friends. You are approaching the
Aquarian Age.* Mundane existence is about to change to spiritual context!

I must admit that these thoughts are *far beyond* what I
started with in 1947 when the saucers came to Waterloo, Iowa,
the same week that we moved to that city. Like a few others at
that time, I was *merely curious!* Then came the excitement of
their being *wherever I was about to be* in a few weeks — always
just ahead of me. Then the developing interest which was
nothing more than "if I could only see one!" Then the whole
family saw four at once, playing around with lights and movements such as nothing Earth has produced even thirty years
later! Then the search for "what they were," followed by "why
are they here?"

When my wife saw one up close to our house while I was sleep-
ing, a ship as big as a water tower, I began to wonder "why the
interest in our family?" Later came the knowledge that we were
not the only ones to whom this was happening. And finally, a
skeptical acceptance that they were landing, picking up earth
plants and animals — and then the *contacts* and the *communication* with thousands of normal, well-respected people!

At the same time all this was happening, I was learning in all
these other fields, with many helpful people in our Club that
were beginning to develop unusual "gifts." Organic gardening,
without the use of poisonous pesticides and herbicides. Psychic
phenomena which were not too different from the "appearing
and disappearing saucers." Then "life after death" and the
"communication with former friends and relatives," still called
"works of the devil" by people who completely misunderstand
the whole concept of "life on the other side" and think only in
terms of "heaven" and "hell." Then the (at first repulsive) idea
of reincarnation, the reasons for it, and the understanding of
many things that seemed inconsistent, if not unjust, before.
Now *everything* seems to be "complete law and order!"

There were many side issues, related but maybe not important enough to include here. But actually, after 22 years of the
normal educational process, 1947 started a new learning process

that now seems as normal and progressive as starting anew in kindergarten, and going through a whole course of study until a new university, consisting of many "colleges" is the end result.

To those metaphysical students to whom this is old stuff, my purpose is to show the inter-relatedness of *all things,* including orthodox church services, which are part of the curriculum for those who are satisfied there. And "normal educational processes" for those who are satisfied there, as long as "academia" does not become an end in itself and produce many "blind spots" in one's continuing "education." (Many scholars find this the hardest bit of knowledge to accept, because it was not in their academic curriculum — and sometimes threatens their "Ph.D. degree information.") Most of all let me suggest, "Don't fall into the same pit that orthodoxy did, and battle one another as though *Yours* was the *only* way!"

And to those to whom most of these concepts are new, and maybe unacceptable, I would say that you should simply remember that it has taken me almost forty years of study while still ministering in a main-line denomination, to arrive at the things stated in this book. Don't be like the eighth-grader, or fourth-grader, who just can't understand the physics or advanced biology that his college brother is talking about. I learned long ago that some of the things I first heard about in this long search had to be "put on the back burner" for a while. Sometimes things have to "simmer" for quite a while even to be palatable! Then, sometimes years later, corroboration would come that *proved to me* that what I had heard years before was a "reasonable fact."

I didn't say it *proved* it to everyone. Each one is on his own "path," and it is immoral to try to force someone else to accept all of his own beliefs.

Throughout my quest, I have never forsaken my love and devotion for Jesus Christ. I *have* learned that "Jesus" and "Christ" are two different things (it isn't his first and last name!) But the fact that "Jesus" and "Christ" were united so completely that Jesus Christ was the perfect God-man is still my firm belief!

I have found many church people who had a thorough church experience throughout their present life who still received a much greater understanding of concepts in the Bible through a study of metaphysics so that their faith became stronger than it ever had been before. To church people to whom the metaphysical concepts are new, let me say that I have had this experience with many people of varying denominations; and invariably they have understood their religion better *after* having studied metaphysics for several years.

Let me suggest for the church person to whom these concepts are new that you might want to read *The Psychic Message of the Scriptures* by T. Rowland Powel, M.A. (Oxon.), with a Foreword by Rev. G. Maurice Elliott. (Copyright 1954 by Omega Press, Reigate, Surrey; printed in Great Britain by Headley Brothers, Ltd., 109 Kingsway, London WC2 and Ashford Kent.)

In the Foreword Rev. Elliott says: "*The Psychic Message of the Scriptures* will bring untold relief and joy into the lives of a large number of men and women in the Christian Church and outside it who, although interested in psychical phenomena, have not yet connected them with similar happenings recorded in Holy Scripture, which they have regarded as altogether outside our range of experience *today.*

"Mr. Powel's work is a 'bridge' across which we may travel between This World and That. The book will help to make the Book of Books understandable, real and vital to the reader. Much Biblical narrative hitherto deemed incredible on the ground that 'nothding like it happens today' becomes credible and, indeed, vibrant with life in the hands of our author. His essay will encourage men and women to open their Bibles once again and to read them in the light of what is known today to psychic scientists whose findings are so well presented to us in this book.

"Many will live to thank God for its message, which will have solved for them (. . . .) important and insistent questions (as, 'Why don't miracles happen *today?*' 'Where are the 'signs and wonders' *today?*' 'If Jesus promised that we should 'do the works that He did and greater works,' why are they not done *today?*')

"I (wish the book and its great message Godspeed), feel(ing) sure that it will bring enlightenment and understanding to all who read it."

Let me go back now to the changes that might result in society if these ancient truths were taught regularly, from childhood on, and were accepted as freely as the theory of evolution is taught in our educational process.

Fundamental to this change in thinking is the idea that "God is within" (we are 'made in his spiritual image' — Genesis 1:27), rather than *up there somewhere,* and *far away!*

God is not real to many people. Just notice how people suddenly are aware of their language when a minister walks into a group of people who have been taking the Lord's Name "in vain!" God was there all the time, but they were not aware of that. When they know a minister is around, even if he is *not* the "stuffed shirt" type, they suddenly *become* aware! We are subject to our five senses, and therefore judge God (and heaven) in that manner. This *change of thinking* makes people aware of the whole spiritual world about them!

What would happen to crime, war, acts of violence and illicit sex, and many other little personal sins if *everyone* became aware of the thousands of ordinarily invisible people that interlace with our physical world? The *Universe* is not what the astronomers describe: it is that, *plus* what the metaphysical students know exists in another dimension. And while "they" are too busy to simply sit next to us and *stare* at each act we do, I learned long ago that they *do know* when loved ones of theirs stray from the straight and narrow. And "they" are often involved as loving guides to help steer us to a better way, although there is a *law* that "they" dare not interfere with our free will. The fact is expressed in the popular song, *I Did It My Way,* that we have to learn by our own mistakes!

When I say "they," I refer, of course, to the deceased who are living in a world of their own, and doing the Father's Will there.

There are many things to do there. My grandfather, who once lived among the Pennsylvania coal miners, was at a later time involved (in "heaven") with helping people who had just "come over there" because of a mine explosion. I remember one time he told me (at night) that there were *no survivors* in a particular mine explosion that had been on the news just a few hours before that. On the news broadcast they still had hope that they would find some alive when they got to them. But *my grandfather was right: There were no survivors,* when help finally got through.

Grandfather ought to know! He was there helping them understand what happened to them, and getting them acclimated to their new environment!

But there are also people here in this world, living in the flesh, who can "see into" and "hear" in the invisible, inaudible world, while still in their own flesh bodies. They have gifts that have been earned through lifetimes of service! Now these people are often called by police to help solve crimes. By describing "where they 'see' the body," the police can find the body and thereby have other clues by which they can find the culprit who committed the crime! I have known several such people in my own investigations of psychic phenomena. What if all potential criminals were aware of these facts?

There is another way that conditions would change if reincarnation and "self-judgment" were a part of everyone's knowledge and belief system. People do not like the idea of God as a Big Man with a White Beard, sitting on an immense White Throne, dishing out judgment to one individual after another, saying: "You are fit for heaven," and to the next, "You go to hell." Where do you think that latter phrase came from in our street vernacular? *From that very misconception of God!*

But what if, after you die, you had to watch what might be likened to a movie of your whole past life ("Akashic Records"), and saw for yourself what your repeated mistakes were?

What if you had to judge yourself, and decide for yourself how you would best learn to conquer the problems you saw needed to be conquered?

And what if the Karmic Board let you decide what kind of a home, environment, race and nation you would next be born into, in order to meet the consequences that would teach you the needed lessons? They might counsel you as to what kind of environment would help you learn the lessons of hatred versus love, prejudice versus understanding, poverty versus wealth, violence versus patience, prostitution versus a happy family life, and the kind of religious faith that would best help you in all these problesm — *but they would not force you.* If you want to repeat your same mistakes and "bang your head against a stone wall" once more, that is your choice — *your judgment —* but with all the loving help that you might need to make your decision! I imagine that you would not care to live life, with all its mistakes and heartaches, *just as you have lived it this time!* And *you don't have to!*

But if you knew beforehand that this was the process, would you make all the mistakes, and perform all the "sins" that you did this time? Why not try to be as "good" as possible, with the Example and Help of our Savior, Jesus Christ, instead of being as obdurate and perverse as possible, and going through this purgatory and hell of remorse of your own making? "Hell" may not seem real to many people; but most have experienced some degree of remorse. Would you like a hundred years of that?

I say "a hundred years of that" just as an example. But the Earth time involved in such corrective procedure is usually that long or longer between lifetimes — although there are instances where it occurs more quickly.

But think of the "Plans" involved! Arrangements have to be made with certain individuals to "be your parents" the next time (and maybe they have had to make arrangements with the individuals who were to be *their* parents — your grandparents). Maybe your grandparents the next time are already born, having made their arrangements previously, but *your new parents* still have to be born, and grow up, *before you can be born!* Then *you* have to grow up before conditions are right to marry the person, for instance, that you want to meet again to "finish the karma" with that person (which can be helpful to both of you, if handled correctly this time).

I say all these things to be sure you understand that *you are your own judge,* because only *you* know what you eventually want to be. That is, what we call your "Higher Self" knows; but the *mortal* experiences add to that which each 'personality' derives from life!

Meditation is a way for your mortal phase, your "lower self," your "ego" to come into harmony with that Higher Self. That is why so many people who meditate recommend "going within" to find *your* way. This is the difference between seeing God as only *Out There,* or seeing Him/Her/It *Within!*

I think of God as similar to a Fourth of July "sparkler," with individual "sparks" having been placed in each of us. There is still the Divine Source, and *Prayer* is relating to that Divine Source. But meditation is the individual "spark" remembering that it is a piece of the original *whole.*

This may be a poor illustration, but it is one that has been helpful to me. I don't suppose even the Masters and Swamis and Yogis can *completely* describe *all* the attributes of God (otherwise *they* would be God). They are sometimes referred to as "gods," but this has a different connotation to me.

Homosexuality is getting an increasing amount of attention these days, in education, politics and even in the church. Students of "psychic readings" into past lives tell us that this problem has often been caused by a too sudden changing of sexes — that is, the person may have been in a condition of hatred for the opposite sex, and the only way for him/her to discover and learn what the opposite sex went through in their experiences was *to be a member of the opposite sex!*

So the person decided, or was "counseled," to enter the fetus of the sex opposite to what he/she had been for so long. But if the preparations for such a sudden change were not adequate, the person might be entirely unwilling to accept the change after arriving here. Homosexuality results.

Here is another re-thinking society ought to do. The homosexual tries to persuade everybody that "he/she can't help it that he/she was born with these tendencies." Homosexuals often try to convince the rest of us, rather than looking at themselves, going to a "reader" or "hypnotist in past life experiences," to find out *why* their tendencies originated, and to accept the fact that *they made this decision themselves, and ought to accept their own decision.*

Gina Cerminara, a doctor of psychology, studied the Edgar Cayce past life readings in her doctorate work. Her book, *Many Mansions,* is well worth reading by anyone with a sexual, marital, financial, or religious hang-up!

Another good book to help understand oneself and the situation he/she is in is Dick Sutphen's *You Were Born Again to be Together.* Or any number of Brad Steiger's books on this or related subjects.

It is entirely believable that in this day when society is gradually changing from a male-dominated society to one where equality is the norm, some of our homosexuals might have made this sex-change as a *volunteer* to help us in this transition! If so — and they understood this — their attitude about it would change — and our attitude toward them ("homophobia") would also change!

After all, this attitude about a change in sexual roles has been coming about gradually during the past half century! Though men used to wear wigs, fancy pants, silk shirts, and perfume, the women began doing that so long ago that most people even forgot that men started it.

Next, women took to wearing pants, and bobbing their hair, a "male" characteristic until recently. When our young men began to be more sensitive (a "female" trait), they let their hair grow longer, and were not quite as afraid to be seen crying. When a woman was earning most of the livelihood, making more money than hubby, it was less onerous for him to do housework and even stay home and take care of the kids. Many such

changes have been coming on gradually, as more women take
"men's roles" in society, and men become less fearful of admitt-
ing to some feminine characteristics. It is simply a matter of
balancing the scales that have been out of balance too long.

If *this* has been going on for a century, could the planning
ahead "on the other side," before birth, also have included
changing sexes for the same purpose? If so, let's accept it for
what it is, and not pretend it's something else!

None of this is meant to accept the unnatural *sexual acts,* but
simply the sexual *tendencies or characteristics.* While homosexuals may *think* their sexual *acts* are "natural" for them, that
must be reconsidered in the light of the *reason for their having
homosexual tendencies, as suggested in the above possibilities.*

In her *Reflections From an Angel's Eye,* Francie Steiger has
channeled from her angel the fact that all people can receive
visions of a *personal* nature by engaging in daily meditation.
Prophets and Holy Men sometimes receive visions of *Universal
Teachings.* But most individuals receive visions of a personal
nature, to help him on his own path. Each one's path is different, for no two souls have had identical backgrounds in all lifetimes. Most individual visions are for *that* person, since that
person's Higher Self knows what *that* person needs. But what
guidance might pertain to one, may not at all apply to others.

> *Those who channel Personal Truths and attempt to
> force their understandings upon others have violated the
> free will of masses of people and prevented millions from
> discovering their OWN personal awarenesses from their
> angelic guidance.*

Why do we have so many "faiths" and so many "denominations?" Well, for one thing, different leaders of spiritual truths
have been given *universal* truths, but bathed in the consciousness and mores of the society for which it was given, and at
different times in history. But there may also be Personal
Truths which were misinterpreted by the visionary as Universal Truths — and he tried to force everyone else into *that* mode.
Again, from Francie Steiger's book:

> *We have all perhaps wondered why one spiritual leader
> will issue one kind of proclamation while another decrees a
> widely disparate revelation. The answer lies in the fact*

that they were disclosing Personal Truths, visions of a personal nature which were meant ESPECIALLY, and only, for the RECEIVER of them. Such private insights were NEVER intended to be proclaimed to the masses, for they would only cause men and women to set aside their OWN paths to God and to attempt to follow the path of another.

Many a religious leader, misled by some personal revelation, and many popular T.V. preachers ought to be aware of this Universal Metaphysical Truth, as found again in Francie Steiger's angelic teaching, reported in her book:

I consider it a great violation against individual spiritual sovereignty when certain hierarchal members of organized religious bodies have discouraged men and women from seeking personal contact with angelic beings and with the heavenly realm. We are each to receive our own personal awareness that aid us in fulfilling our purpose in being, our mission. We must never attempt to pull anyone onto our PERSONAL path to God, for that is a violation of free will, his or her purpose of existence. It is an offense to the Divine Plan of God to interfere with another's way of going.

This is *exactly* what the Space Brothers have told many communicators in dozens of transmissions. Maybe this is another reason they are here, the correction of many of our "religious" ideas! Remember the MIRO group I referred to earlier (Military-Industrial-Religious-Oligarchy)? Here is the "Religious" part of the "Silence Group" talked about by so many UFO investigators. (Do you have any idea who the "Men In Black" might be?)

There are all stripes of religious leaders who through spiritual ignorance, spiritual naiveté, or a deliberate effort to control their congregations, give fearful admonitions to their people: "revelatory visions were given *only* to sainted ones of old," or "you might be fooled by the Devil or one of his angels and be condemned to eternal damnation."

I have been similarly warned myself by people who suppose they have more of the "baptism of the Holy Spirit" than I have. It is just as logical to ask whether *they* are not perhaps "being fooled by the Devil."

I am not throwing aspersions on the charismatic movement,

but let me just say that I have been in *many* of their meetings
where "the Holy Spirit" was their *only* explanation of what was
happening. In some cases I could just as logically have assign-
ed the "other tongues" they were speaking to "memories of
former lifetimes when they spoke in different tongues." Or, according to the results that happened afterward as they caused
"divisiveness in the household of God" I could have also judged
that "they were being fooled by the Devil!" Still another explanation *could* be "possession by a spirit of a deceased person of another nationality."

Let me state that the heavenly realms, or the "realms of the
Highest Vibration" are beautiful beyond description! My
mother was an accomplished musician. Upon her passing she
reported hearing music more beautiful than any she had ever
heard before! And the beauty there surpasses that of what the
Space Brothers and our own astronauts describe as "the Beautiful Planet," our Earth. Francie Steiger reports the same:

> *The beauty of the place appears even more vivid and*
> *tangible than that of Earth. There are beautiful trees and*
> *thick vegetation. The flowers are vibrant with color and*
> *appear as though dunked in plush velvet. You will feel as*
> *one with all living things.*
>
> *You will see a sparkling river of cool water, and it will re-*
> *fresh, as well as cleanse, your entire being within and with-*
> *out, before you approach it. You will watch playful animals*
> *frolicking nearby, and you will become one with their child-*
> *like vibrations . . . The sensations are so pleasurable that*
> *you will be almost overwhelmed.*
>
> *. . . unconditional love will permeate your entire being . . .*
> *the freedom that this love offers you is unsurpassed by any*
> *other love that you have ever known.*

This is just the same as hundreds of people have experienced
who have had the "death experience" and returned to tell about
it, as reported by many serious researchers, *and by personal*
friends of mine who have gone through the same experience.

This "heavenly feeling" is a thing to look forward to. it cannot adequately be described! But those who have gone through
it *never again fear death!* However, they also realize that one
cannot short-cut entrance to that experience. A Light Being always tells them to go back, "it is not time yet for you to stay." So

suicide or murder to attain it merely brings the remorse that one did not complete the karma with the people with whom he made all those advance preparations for coming here that have been described before. *But the "Heavenly Experience" can be experienced in meditation,* and Francie gives details of *how* to achieve that blissful state in your moments of meditation.

CHAPTER 16

The New Age of Aquarius

YEARS AGO I read Velikovsky's two books, *Worlds in Collision* and *Ages in Chaos*. I was impressed with the number of fields of research with which he was acquainted. In all my schooling in traditional education I don't ever remember seeing a book with as many footnotes! He quoted from many fields of research. He even confused the intellectuals, who were also his greatest critics. (I felt at times that the criticism was founded on jealousy over the profundity of his range.) Years later another author came out with a book the name of which was something like *Velikovsky Revisited*. These untraditional views were being given more credence by some scholars due to some of the discoveries in our Space Age.

In her book, *The Aquarian Conspiracy,* Marilyn Ferguson speaks a great deal about "Paradigm Shifts," where "new perspectives give birth to new historic ages."

"We discovered the uses of fire and the wheel, language and writing. We found that the earth only *seems* solid. We learned to communicate, fly, explore."

And each one of these changes in the "frameworks of thought" made complete changes in history from that time on. These new paradigms are like the "hidden pictures" in the main picture in a child's book of puzzles. They are "hidden" only until we once see that there are "pictures within the main picture." Then we see the hidden pictures every time we look at the main picture again.

Copernicus, Galileo, Pasteur and Mesmer are examples of discoverers who made an intuitive leap without yet having all the data in place, and who therefore were greeted with coolness, or even mockery and hostility. It was not until much later that their ideas were accepted and made a part of the "new paradigm."

The "Ancient Truth" contained in this book of mine was regarded just like that forty years ago! Western Civilization had lost the ancient truths in the Middle Ages, or what has been called "the Dark Ages."

The flying saucers, for me and for thousands, began a new Paradigm Shift, and a whole new "history"; for while the world *seems* to some to be getting worse in its immorality in many fields, at the same time *thousands, tens of thousands,* are seeing life in this Greater Universe more interesting and exciting than ever — and *leading to "something" that we do not yet fully comprehend.*

Brad Steiger once said that it is as great a leap as when Neanderthal Man became *Homo Sapiens.* I asked him what he would call the new man, and he replied, "Perhaps *Homo Spiritus!*"

Ferguson says that there are four basic ways in which we change our minds:

1. CHANGE BY EXCEPTION. Our old belief system remains intact but allows for a handful of anomalies.
2. INCREMENTAL CHANGE occurs bit by bit, and the individual is not aware of having changed.
3. PENDULUM CHANGE, the abandonment of one closed and certain system for another. The hawk becomes the dove, the disenchanted religious zealot becomes an atheist, the promiscuous person turns into a prude, etc.
4. PARADIGM CHANGE — transformation . . . the fourth dimension of change: the new perspective, the insight that allows the information to come together in a new form or structure . . . In many ways, it is the most challenging kind of change because it relinquishes certainty. It allows for different interpretations from different perspectives at different times.

I have seen every one of these four types of change in others in my lectures around the country. I think my own change could be categorized under the second, *Incremental Change,* at least in the beginning. The "anomalies" were the flying saucers for me: others began at a different place and with other subject-matter.

As a minister, trained for the job in the traditional manner, and with three authentic degrees from well-known college and

theological schools, it was definitely *not* a "pendulum change."
Nor was it merely a "change by exception." I researched UFOs
in a more scientific manner than the Condon Committee,
which started out with a definite purpose, funded by the government, and which ignored all the *facts* that would not fit into
that purpose. (This could not be called "scientific" by any
stretch of the imagination!)

No, my change came about "bit by bit," accepting *only* what
did not interfere with my basic training — and *yet* accepting
what did differ from my education *when the proof was there!*
After all, Boston University School of Theology, where I spent
more years than anywhere else in school, *taught me to think for
myself!* Then when I did just that, a letter from a respected professor advised me to "stick to the traditional approach" that I
had learned from him and others in that particular field! (This
was ten years after I was in the ministry in Iowa.)

"Bit by bit" I changed, not radically, but "piece by piece." But
after several lectures on one subject to the same people in my
church (which they enjoyed, applauded and agreed with), I
would *continually* discover by their discussions in classes afterward that it was *not* a *Paradigm Change!* Theirs was still the
"old belief system remaining intact, allowing for a handful of
anomalies." Of course they were in their sixties; but *so was I at
the time I was teaching the classes!*

And in my "flying saucer lectures" at noon luncheon clubs,
which I mentioned before, they were interested in "the anomaly
only during the speech" — no carry-over for business or personal life!

It must be apparent to the reader by now, however, that at
present mine is a *Paradigm Change* — an almost complete
transformation from my former mode of thought. And hopefully to fit into the new Aquarian Age!

In the prior 67 years from this writing the United States has
been involved in three major wars and at least three "police
actions" which were the same as wars! I realize that some of
these were brought on by the "people in control" of presidents
and Congress — the MIRO group mentioned before. But please,
can't we quit calling ourselves a "peace-loving nation"? Six
wars in 67 years is one in almost every decade!

When a war does come along, no matter how bizaree the circumstances, one always hears men saying, "I had to go. Let
those d— conscientious objectors go, too. And the guys who flee

to Canada." Does that sound as though even the citizens are "peace-loving"? It almost sounds as if, instead of saying "we're all in the same boat" (which we are), they are saying in effect, "Let them all, these younger guys, get into the same boat I'm in, *even if it is sinking!*

Here's another thing that will change! We have been informed that there are many Atlanteans here now *who have never reincarnated since that time.* Are they the ones that push toward the nuclear holocaust, which was probably responsible for the sinking of Atlantis, according to those who read the Akashic records?

But at the same time there are soldiers from the "Hundred Years' War" as well as recent wars who have reincarnated at this time. This may explain why we are having more conscientious objectors and "peaceniks" and "draft dodgers" than ever before! They saw the futility of war "from the other side," and they are back to stop this silly Earthian habit.

The Space People say they have outlawed war millenia ago. They dare not *force* us to abandon our warlike motivations (they cannot abandon "free will" as a learning experience for all sentient beings). But they certainly are not allowing us to take our warlike propensities out into space. We are trying, with our "Model T" space vehicles, but they have "time travel" and many other modes of travel that have already shown us that our 17,000 miles per hour is S L O W ! *We are quarantined on this planet* (the Moon is just a skip and a jump!) until we, too, outlaw war, and approximate their spirituality (*Living* their beliefs, not just *Talking* their "religion")!

The Fourth Dimension, into which the saucers disappear and from which materializations of all kinds appear, is admitedly hard to understand. And especially so when "time" as we know it is different. There is a Victorian fantasy called *Flatland* which might illustrate the difficulty one might have in understanding it who has not had the experience of reaching into that dimension.

Flatland was a two-dimensional world. As the story opens, the narrator, a middle-aged *square,* has a disturbing dream in which he visits a one-dimensional realm, *Lineland.* Here the inhabitants can move only from point to point, or in other words "on a line." Marilyn Ferguson tells about it further in her *Aquarian Conspiracy:*

With mounting frustration SQUARE attempts to explain

himself — that he is a Line of Lines, from a domain where you can move not only from point to point but also from side to side. The Angry Linelanders are about to attack him when he awakens.

Does this sound like what happened to people who, forty years ago, tried to explain their encounters with saucers, or ghosts, or out-of-body experiences to the rest of us? Marilyn Ferguson continues:

Later that same day SQUARE attempts to help his grandson, a LITTLE HEXAGON, with his studies. The grandson suggests the possibility of a Third Dimension — a realm with up and down as well as side to side. The SQUARE proclaims this notion foolish and unimaginable.

That very night the SQUARE has an extraordinary, life-changing encounter: a visit from an inhabitant of SPACE-LAND, the realm of Three Dimensions.

Another step in our "saucer encounters" — a person who heard of UFO's but didn't believe in this hokum finally sees one, or even has an encounter of the second kind, seeing one, landed on the ground, which actually stops his car so that neither radio, lights or ignition will work! He is frightened out of his wits.

Now back to the Victorian fantasy, *Flatland:*

At first the SQUARE is merely puzzled by his visitor, a peculiar circle who seems to change in size, even disappear. The visitor explains that he is a SPHERE. He only seemed to change size and disappear because he was moving toward the SQUARE in Space and descending at the same time.

Explanations by UFO researchers do not reach the person who has had these experiences. He cannot yet understand what happened either to him or to his automobile (or airplane!) He only knows it was "weird"! And very frightening!

Realizing that argument alone will not convince SQUARE of the Third Dimension, the exasperated SPHERE creates for him and experience of DEPTH. The

SQUARE is badly shaken.:
>   *There was a dizzy, sickening sensation of sight that*
> *was not seeing; I saw a Line that was no Line; Space*
> *that was not Space. I was myself and not myself.*
> *When I could find voice, I shrieked aloud in agony,*
> *"Either this is madness or it is Hell."*
>   *"It is neither," calmly replied the voice of the*
> *SPHERE. "It is Knowledge; it is THREE DIMEN-*
> *SIONS. Open your eyes once again and try to look*
> *steadily."*
>   *Having had an insight into another dimension, the*
> *SQUARE becomes an evangelist, attempting to convince*
> *his follow FLATLANDERS that Space is more than just a*
> *wild notion of mathematicians. Because of his insistence*
> *he is finally imprisoned, for the public good. Every year*
> *thereafter the high priest of FLATLAND, the CHIEF CIR-*
> *CLE, checks with him to see if he has regained his senses,*
> *but the stubborn SQUARE continues to insist that there is*
> *a third dimension. He cannot forget it, he cannot explain it.*

Exactly this has happened in *this* period of time! Rudolph
Hess, who was imprisoned *before* World War II was well under-
way, and who was probably not responsible for the Nazi atroci-
ties, *has been kept in the Spandau Prison* for more than
thirty-five years. He knows something the Russian authorities
do not want him to tell, for it is the U.S.S.R. that insists that he
not be released.

An airplane pilot who was taken into a large UFO, airplane
and all, was put into "asylum" for telling such a story, although
authorities checked *and he could not have stayed in the air as
long as he did with the amount of gas he carried!*

Many others have been put under psychiatric care because
they could not explain to our *Flatlanders* what happened to
them in their Fourth Dimension experiences. Contactees have
been taken into *solid* ships, taken to some far-away place, explaining that they had been on the moon, to Venus, Mars, etc.,
even describing what space looked like ten years before our first
"astronauts" told us the same thing!

How do you care to explain it? Could ship, Earth, people and
all have gone into the Fourth Dimension — as did the ship that
weighed so much near Jefferson, South Dakota, that it injured
the highway, yet disappeared over my friend's car, becoming a

"mist" like a cloud? No wonder we *Flatlanders* do not believe them. And we won't until, like *Square,* we are taken into the dimension of *depth* — and then we won't be able to explain it to the rest of the *Flatlanders!*

What is most interesting is how those in a Victorian Age came to write such a fantasy as has *actually happened* in the third quarter of this century! Probably in the same way that the famous Dean Jonathan Swift told us about the *two satellites* that encircle Mars more than a hundred years before our astronomers "discovered" them, even giving their approximate size and distance from the planet. About Dean Swift's information, the *Encyclopedia Americana* says it was "the most astonishing prophecy of the past thousand years as to whose full authenticity there is no shadow of doubt."

Lillian Bau Nothdurft, who materialized before the author in 1954 or 1956 in Anderson, Indiana, and reminded him of how much she loved him. She had been seen in the late '50's by Bernyce, near our piano in the Maquoketa, Iowa parsonage, though not recognized at that time for who she was. She had died before we met, and at that time Bernyce had not seen any pictures. Later she visited with Bernyce in her dreams when we needed family advice. It was not until relatives sent us pictures of my mother that my wife was SURE that that was the person she had been visiting with many nights!

CHAPTER 17

Nature Out of Control

ISN'T IT STRANGE how inconsistent we are? We have read many times that "In the beginning God created the heaven and the earth" (Genesis 1:1) and several times the writer says, "and God saw that it was good." We see "God's creation" all about us, and often call it that.

Yet when we see strange things in nature, we name them something other than *God's* creation. In northeast Iowa, we have the *Devil's* Backbone State Park. In eastern Wyoming, the *Devil's* Tower. In northern Arizona, *Hell's* Canyon; and in southern Arizona, the *Devil's* Road. All over the nation we name things after the *Devil* rather than after *God!*

Then when something *bad* comes along, like an earthquake, a flood, a crop-destroying hailstorm, an eighteen-inch snow fall, or a ten-inch rainstorm, insurance companies call it *an act of God!*

We'd better get our metaphysics straightened out! *God* doesn't do all these bad things. *WE DO!*

The "elementals" are tired of man's manipulation of his fellow man for selfish purposes, and they are out of control *because man is out of control!* It is *chaotic thought, over centuries of time,* that causes nature to act up — not just the "shooting of guns and artillery" during major wars. *Man's thoughts* are wrong prior to, during, and after wars! Nature will not tolerate this much longer.

Since our multiplication of wars during this century, nature has gotten more and more out of hand. Man is contantly at war against his fellow man, and treats nature as his enemy "to be conquered and manipulated." Several countries for the last few years have been engaged in "weather war" against each other — and "psychotronic warfare" as well. But none will admit this, even though our weather constantly is called by meteorologists "the worst of the century," or "the worst since records have been kept." Every winter headlines in the newspapers proclaim, "the worst ever" or the "worst in fifty years."

Jesus showed how man can control nature *by the right attitude toward God and fellow man!* It is no mystery how he fed five thousand with five loaves and two fishes, or how he stilled the storm at sea, or even how his own body was raised from death in the tomb! We can't duplicate those feats, but it is only because *we do not duplicate his attitudes toward all of life and creation.* Even the drying up of a fig tree overnight was done for a teaching purpose. *Anyone who lived the kind of life he lived has the right to use nature as he did — and to continue to live after they killed him!*

I have seen evidences of American Indians who were so in tune with nature, not opposing it but working with it, that when rain was necessary for survival, *the rains came!* The White Man has a lot to *learn* from the Indians, instead of looking down on them as a "backward people!" Our attitude of superiority toward anyone unlike ourselves has caused all sorts of trouble for them, and for us!

And this is the same attitude that keeps us from accepting the *fact* that the Flying Saucers are *far superior to us,* both in technology and in spiritual acumen! We have a "mass inferiority complex," and inferiority complexes usually show up by trying to emphasize our good points while de-emphasizing that which outshines us. Or as some have said, "cutting the other fellow down to his knees to make ourselves look taller!"

If we *studied* the Indians, or the yogis, or others who know metaphysical principles, we could have a civilization that would again be *The Golden Age!* And that is coming. Those who can't take those vibrations — or refuse to live by correct metaphysical principles — will simply not be able to stay around. They will "take themselves out of here" by one method or another!

CHAPTER 18

Is The Study of Metaphysics "Practical"?

WE HAVE mentioned one practical result that happened in our "Cup and Saucer Club." When we studied different aspects — and individuals realized they were part of a sympathetic group — talents and "gifts" began to emerge that they were not aware they had before this. These were practical things that helped them in their work.

Another practical aspect is one's own safety, as when one is "guided," or "prodded" *not* to take a certain train or plane, which consequently has a wreck or crashes, killing many on board. Explanation has already been given about possible reasons for most passengers being killed, while only a few are "warned." And there may have been others who were "warned" but paid no attention.

Those who are in groups who study *how* these warnings are given, and *by whom,* are much more likely to pay attention when they feel the urge not to go on a vehicle. Those who got the urge, but paid no attention to it, are no longer around to tell us whether or not they had such warnings. But the ones who were saved by such warnings *are.* Example: those who were warned to stay off the "unsinkable *Titanic*" and *did* stay off.

Still another practical application is in "finding a parking place" when needed in a hurry. I have done this so many dozens of times that it just couldn't be called "coincidence" any more. And so have many of my metaphysical friends.

I always pray, or "throw the idea out into the ethers," that somewhere near where I have to go in a hurry to make a short stop, *someone* who is through with their business but is a little "pokey" will be "urged" to leave so I will be getting there at about the time they back out. But if I am courteous enough even with my invisible friends to say, "It isn't that important this time," often I *do* have to hunt a while. But in the cases when the need *is* urgent, someone almost always backs out just as I am coming to the place I need to stop. As I say, this has happened dozens of times!

On occasion a carload of ministers has been on the way together to a Pastors' School or other church meeting. As is the usual thing, all kinds of discussions take place on such trips, including safety on the road. One minister in particular surprised me with his *lack* of knowledge of metaphysics, or just plain *prayer answers*. He stated that he didn't think it did any good to pray for safety on the road; one should just be as careful as possible.

How many times I have prayed, "Father, if you foresee any danger up ahead, please urge me either to speed up or slow down, so that we are not there at the time an accident might have happened."

Sometimes I find myself unconsciously doing just that — speeding up for a few miles or slowing down for no reason that I know of. All of a sudden I am *aware* that I have slowed down, even when I had been using the cruise control before that. I don't know whether that is *the reason* I slowed down; but I do know that that is *how* our invisible friends sometimes give us a nudge through the unconscious.

But my pastor friend thought that, since you can't foresee what is going to happen at a certain intersection, for instance, you *can't* avoid an accident that is inevitable. Maybe this Methodist believes in predestination, I don't know.

To those who might read this book and remember a terrible auto accident I once had, let me say that I now know *why* I had that accident; but I also know that my invisible friends *kept it from killing me!* A nurse was on the scene in moments, and a doctor came by a few moments later and gave me a shot to prevent shock.

When I got to town the doctor at the hospital X-rayed me twice because he couldn't believe that with all the multiple fractures I had that a broken rib had not punctured my lung, for their were several ribs that had two broken ends!

An important side-light on that accident and my "protective guides" follows. I said I now know *why* the accident happened; it was a tremendously important learning experience. And several things about it seem too strange to be mere coincidence.

It happend on April 17, 1959 — the twenty-fifth anniversary of my mother's death, *exactly, to the day!* Not only that, but I was *exactly* as old on that day as she was when she died! Yet, I *did not die!* But I am sure they spared me from having one of those several loose ribs puncture my lung or heart! *And here I am, writing about it exactly fifty years after her death,* April 17, 1934!

Several years later I was our Annual Conference delegate to Rust College in Mississippi.'I combined that journey with an extra week of vacation — in Missouri and at Mardi Gras in New Orleans. On my way back I encountered ice on the road within twenty miles of home.

Even though I was careful, when I rounded a curve the car spun around and headed for the ditch and a plowed field beyond — *not frontwards, but backwards!* There was no way to steer in that position. I recalled my former accident in an immediate flash of memory and yelled aloud, *"Oh, no — Not again!"*

Believe it or not, the car went *straight backward for a hundred yards,* and came to a halt. I drove straight ahead and got back on the road, getting home without further incident! Later I learned through conversations with my grandfather in spirit that they heard me and saw to it that the car did not turn over! *My yell was the same as a prayer, and that prayer was answered!*

The *timing* of the first incident, and of my writing about it, did not occur to me at all until this book was half-finished!

Are my Invisible Mother/Grandfather still guiding me in the writing of this Aquarian Age book? It would be hard for me to think otherwise!

Incidentally, my wife has visited with them in her dreams. She knew my grandfather in life, but she had never seen my mother or a picture of her. But when we finally obtained a picture of Mother from relatives, Bernyce was sure that was who it was — only much younger looking now! People "on the other side" do not "age"; they grow *back* to the *prime of life,* although they sometimes appear to people *as they knew them* so that they will recognize them.

Evidence of the *un-practicality* of *not* studying metaphysics is found in our nation's having lowered the age of "adult hood!" It has always been 21 until recently, when it was lowered to 18. But we discovered by sad experience that one cannot change the real age of a person by just changing the figures! We paid a dear price in lives lost by letting 18-year-olds drink alcohol and decide for themselves many other things. As a result of this mistake along this line we not only have many more lives lost and insurance rates 'way up, but we also have younger and younger people taking drugs and alcohol and entering sexual activity because many of the "adult" 18-year-olds were still in high school. All kinds of trouble has resulted from changing the "adulthood" age.

There was a metaphysical reason for 21 being the age of adulthood. Every cell in our bodies changes every seven years. Great changes take place in the physical structure at about age seven, and again at fourteen. Three of these seven-year periods bring the age to 21, and no amount of legislation can change the way God made us.

Notice that both the number three and the number seven are very mystical numbers all through the Bible. We even have seven "chakras" or places in the physical body where matter and spirit join. Three times seven is twenty-one, *not* eighteen. Legislators are belatedly trying to change our mistake from eighteen to nineteen. This still is not right, and they had better start learning the practical-ness of metaphysical laws of living.

The old cliche is, "If a fellow is old enough to fight, he's old enough to drink." How fallacious! Better it would be if we did not allow him to fight either, until he was twenty-one.

If we sent the "old men" to war instead of the immature ones, wars would soon cease! The argument is that the younger men have quicker reflexes. Yes, but the maturity to know that one cannot always depend on one's rapid reflexes does not come for a few more years!

CHAPTER 19

Clouds

A STUDY THAT the reader might find interesting is the use of the word "clouds." The Bible is full of such instances, and the reader should get an exhaustive Concordance and look up all the references to the word "cloud," with their various connotations.

In the first several books of the Old Testament, one finds the implication that the Lord was in a cloud. He led the children of Israel away from Egypt and to the Promised Land by a "pillar of cloud by day and a pillar of fire by night." Clouds covered the mount when Moses went up to the heights to speak with the Lord, and "the Lord called unto Moses out of the midst of the cloud." The tabernacle was covered with a cloud when Moses spoke with the Lord, and Isaiah at a much later times says, "Who are these that fly as a cloud, and as the doves to their windows?"

At the transfiguration of Jesus, after talking to the two "dead" men, Moses and Elijah, "a bright cloud overshadowed them: and behold a voice out of the cloud, which said, 'This is my beloved Son, in whom I am well pleased; hear ye him.' "

When I attended a "materialization séance" with a friend who was a veteran of such experiences and not easily fooled (this was his 80th materialization séance!), I saw numerous "people" both "materialize" and "dematerialize." My mother was one of them, and she has spoken to me privately and on tape since that time.

The "ectoplasm" out of which this materialization is made comes from the medium's body. Such a medium, under controlled conditions, sometimes loses many pounds in weight during the session, and regains it afterward. But the stuff out of which the "bodies" of the "materialized persons" is made looks like a cloud.

Powel, who wrote *The Psychic Message of the Scriptures,* writes that the "ectoplasm out of which the 'bodies' of Moses and Elijah were formed' probably came from the bodies of the three disciples that accompanied Jesus on that mount. Also the "cloud that overshadowed them."

Now, remember the young man near Sioux City, Iowa, who saw the saucer disappear over his car "as a mist." It simply changed dimensions during the short period between the time it left the ground and the time that it was out of sight. It "became a cloud."

A friend of mine from Hiawatha, Iowa, was sitting on a mountain once when a saucer came near the mountain, below him. As he watched, a cloud formed around it while it was sitting still. We were informed later that this was due to the ionization of the air around it, and the partial precipitation that followed. It too "became a cloud" or was enveloped by one (it could be either).

A friend from Portland sent me a picture of a "cloud" near Mt. Shasta. It looked as if it were ready either to "enter the mountain" or as if it was "coming out of the mountain." But it had a shape exactly like the saucers that are like two pie tins, one on the other, one of which is right side up and the other as if the pie tin were turned over on top of the other. There are many pictures of objects that definitely appear to be metal that look like this. But *this one was a cloud!*

Now let me tell you about a "cloud" that was unlike any that anyone has seen before, so far as we know. It was over the San Francisco Peaks *at a height of 100,000 feet!* Now the same article in the paper that told about that, also said that *"no cloud has ever been seen before more than 40,000 feet high!"*

People came from a distance to examine the evidence. I assume, from the way the article read, that they had a good method of estimating its height. It was also *several miles in length* — ten, if my memory serves me correctly. How could a "cloud" exist more than twice as high as "moisture" had ever been seen before? Was it a "Mother Ship?" Clouds have been seen only "less than eight" miles in height, whereas this one was "nearly nineteen miles high!"

No wonder the Indians speak about the San Francisco peaks as "sacred," and resent the ski resorts up there, and resist further encroachment by the white man!

Frank Waters wrote a book called *Book of the Hopi,* which

has information about the Hopi coming to this land, with the help of the Great Spirit as the result of a great flood. This sounds like the story of Noah as found in the Holy Bible, except for the fact that the Hopis had the legend long before the coming of the Spaniards who brought the Bible with them. Our supposition is that the great flood of that time was the "sinking of Lemuria or Mu" which was before the sinking of Atlantis. It makes one think of them as "The Chosen People" of the Western hemisphere!

My copy of *Book of the Hopi* is autographed by "White Bear." Oswald White Bear Fredericks recorded the drawings and source material. He lives in Sedona, Arizona, much of the year. The spokesmen are some thirty elders of the tribe. Their village of Oraibi is indisputably the oldest continuously occupied settlement in the United States. White people ought to lend their support to making this a National Monument. We will someday be amazed at the history of the past that is buried here.

Theirs is a world-view of life, deeply religious in nature. They remind us that we must attune ourselves to the need for inner change if we are to avert a cataclysmic rupture between our own minds and hearts. Now, if ever, is the time for them to talk, for us to listen.

I told earlier of how many times I was in just the right place at just the right time to receive much of the information I have written about in this book. Frank Waters says the same about *Book of the Hopi:*

> This great cooperative effort could not have been obtained before, nor could it be obtained now.

And Frederick H. Howell, writer of the Foreword, says:

> Being in the right place at the right time has won many battles. In this case, another battle has been won. A great people (now few in number indeed) speaks to us, and we are the richer for it if we but have the necessary degree of humility to listen.

Ethnologists have concluded that Hopi ceremonialism is so abstract that it would take longer than a man's lifetime to understand it, and (sic!) *that it required a sixth sense of the Hopis themselves.* Observers of their ceremonies give minute esoteric descriptions of ritual paraphernalia and how they are used. But the esoteric meanings and functions of the ceremonies themselves have remained virtually unknown.

> *This is not wholly due to traditional Hopi secrecy. Professional scientific observers have never granted validity to those aspects of Hopi ceremonialism that border the sixth-sense realm of mysticism. Indeed the rationalism of all the Western world vehemently refutes anything that smacks of the unknown or the "occult." Hence Hopi belief and ceremonialism have been dismissed as the crude folklore and erotic practices of a decadent tribe of primitive Indians which have no relationship to the enlightened tenets of modern civilization.*

This is exactly what we have been saying about why the public either does not believe there are "flying saucers," or does not understand the implications even if they do believe they exist! What about the ten-mile long "cloud," almost nineteen miles high, over the sacred mountains of the Indian tribes (which was part of Hopiland before they were moved again and again, with other tribes encroaching on their territory, also)? Did this "cloud" have anything to do with the spirits that reside in those sacred mountains? These spirits begin to come out shortly after each Winter Solstice. No wonder Indians protest when people desecrate these Holy Mountains with their skiing at this very time of the year! Would you want anyone desecrating the sacred altar of your church?

While this author was in the Heard Museum in Phoenix, looking at Senator Goldwater's famous collection of Kachina dolls (which are being added to constantly), many of which were carved by White Bear, groups of children from the schools were coming through. Each teacher sat them down and explained different things about the dolls. Each teacher had a different story.

I imagine any Hopi, especially White Bear, would have smiled if he could have heard White Teachers' explanations! The senator was emphasized more than White Bear.

Once we were in Sedona, Arizona at a spiritual convention. At one time a channel got up, went into a trance while standing up with his wife's hand upon his shoulder, and gave us a message transmitted directly from a Space Ship. We were told that the town had a different name at one time (easily corroborated), but that the name was changed to *Sedona* because that was the backward spelling of *Anodes*. This had been the spiritual capital of Lemuria.

This is easily understandable when one sees the majestic colored formations of the whole territory and "feels the vibrations there," if sensitive. It was an island off Lemuria at that time. This "safe area" even now seems to include Oraibi and Prescott, Arizona.

Three questions came to mind as we contemplated this information. 1) If Sedona is the *Anodes,* where are the *Cathodes?* 2) Does White Bear, the respected Hopi, know the answer? 3) Does this "Flagship" of the Kachinas which was seen over the San Francisco Peaks have anything to do with the departed spirits, the Hopis, the anodes and the cathodes?

Some day, if I am "in the right place at the right time," maybe the answer to those intriguing questions will come! In the meantime, it is always an exhilarating experience to visit Sedona and Flagstaff. I have now visited Oraibi, too.

CHAPTER 20

Merits of the Traditional Marriage

MANY PEOPLE are living together today in an unwedded state. Now before you ignore this section, let me give you an example or two of what happens to those people at times.

I know several people like that so intimately that the circumstances of their lives are also quite well-known to me. Without pronouncing judgment on them at all, I will simply state some facts.

One young woman was living with a married man who was estranged from his wife, and the two that were just living together became quite attached to each other. In fact, they came to church together, and were thinking about "permanency" but just hadn't gotten around to it. The man became very ill and had to go to a hospital. The young woman suddenly learned that "only immediate family" could see him — and that *she was not immediate family!*

This caused quite an emotional turmoil in her, not to mention what it did to him! She began to think about what would happen if either should die. I do not know whether that is what broke up the arrangement or not, but I do know that she married another person rather soon after all this.

In another case the "arrangement" went on for some time but circumstances began to tell on the relationship because there had not been a permanent tie. Every time one party tried to break the arrangement, the other would lay a "guilt trip" on the first party, and the break-off was not without considerable pain on the part of both. It was not only emotional turmoil for a while but also financial, for one party had done most of the buying for the living arrangements, and the financial settlement was also difficult. The courts could not be brought into it to settle the matter in this case. And the party that had not "provided" much in the arrangement kept pestering the other with phone calls even after moving apart from each other.

Finances cause trouble in married relationships, too; but they are particularly hard to deal with when one party in a "non-marriage" has been used to affluence, and the other has had to exist most of the time in comparative frugality! When no permanent arrangements were made in advance, with *complete* understanding on both sides, then frictions develop on both sides of the fulcrum. All these instances simply come out of a lifetime of dealing with people in a changing world regarding marriage relationships. Many more could be mentioned.

Regarding the marriage relationship, also out of a lifetime of counseling experience, I have come to the definite conclusion that most marriages were subconsciously made for *balance*. But when a couple comes to a third party to try to get an objective view, they rarely see that they balance each other. It has to be pointed out to them, and even then, because they are so *subjectively* involved, they do not always see anything except his or her own viewpoint.

One party is sometimes a spendthrift; the other holds on to money. One likes alcohol or tobacco too much; the other likes neither. One has wild tendencies; the other is quite conservative. One is quite biased; the other more understanding and lenient with others. One might be almost prudish, the other sexually aggressive. One shows emotion outwardly, though not publicly, while the other was raised to show very little emotion. And there are degrees of all these tendencies, some extreme while others are mixed. But they *do* cause tensions! Should marriage be dissolved just because likes and dislikes are so different? There has always been an argument between those who say "like attracts like" and those who say "opposites attract."

The point is that maybe more marriages are "made in heaven" than we realize. When we made those arrangements previously, we realized our own weaknesses and what we needed to learn, and we made the arrangement with one who would make us more balanced in our tendencies. But to some it seems like "hell" to be married to so-and-so, *because they are now involved in the "process" of balancing out the weakness or need.*

Another thing about marriage that I have noticed shows up

in the more advanced age of people. *Companionship* becomes so important then. Most of the people "just living together" are of the younger generation. They are not yet old enough to know the meaning of companionship in the "golden years." I know of one couple that couldn't get along, so they became divorced. When each got into their sixties, they began to have health problems and "went back together" to help each other in their times of need. When either one is sick, the other one is there to take care of them and provide emotional comfort. "The other one thinks enough of me to be with me through this crisis." It really helps!

All these things should be considered (and a whole lot more) by those who tend to "kick over the traces" and throw out all traditional values for what they mistakenly suppose are "the new values." People live from ten to twenty years longer now than they used to when I was growing up. You "younger generation folks" will be among them!

THE CHURCH

It is still true that property values are higher in communities where there are schools and churches. *Why?* Because they still have values, just as they did a hundred years ago! They provide a fellowship that gregarious people (and that's most of us!) need. And the spiritual values that we hear about from Sabbath to Sabbath keep us reminded of "what it's all about!" When a man was bragging about how many acres he owned, a wise person asked him, "Who will own all that in a hundred years from now?"

The trouble is that there are so many viewpoints about the "absolutely right way." We need more *cooperation* than *competition!* And that is the criticism many give for not attending church.

I live in a state that perhaps has more metaphysically-minded people than any other, but I find them to be the same way — thinking that *their particular philosophy* is the way or path to fulfillment or translation or ascension.

Brad Steiger wrote a book called *Psychic City, Chicago.* The Spiritual Frontiers Fellowship movement within the church started there, and we did encounter many psychics in that city. Now the Phoenix-based Omega Spiritual Directory, a metaphysical monthly with a hundred groups supporting it, claims to be one of the best metaphysical papers in the country. Many of these people may find it difficult to "go to church" except in their Phoenix Area "groups." But I hasten to ask, "What is their world-wide mission and program?"

Many of these people know me, and I have attended many of their meetings in various Arizona cities. But I seem to feel like an outsider sometimes. I don't say that it is *because* I am a minister in a mainline denomination; it's probably because it takes time to "prove oneself" in any group.

But I do think that they all must finally come to grips with the question of what their *world-wide program* is. The church has had one for centuries! In fact, the Christian Church would not be in America if St. Paul had not launched out toward the northwest from Palestine, and others followed his missionary zeal!

Paul's "call" came by a metaphysical principle — a dream! (See Acts 16:9) And he met Jesus several times (as I did in 1936!). But he combined metaphysics, his intellectual background under one Gamaliel, and a spiritual zeal for the world. He began churches all over Asia Minor, Greece, and probably Spain and England. Of course we, too, are still in the incipient stages of the Aquarian Age. But we who study the esoteric must have a *world-wide mission* in mind for the future! And connections with Other Worlds!

Churches and synagoges still have their place. And all of us can associate with those of simple faith and those of great knowledge. If you do not find in a church the greater information you seek, start a group of your own — as we did with our Cup and Saucer Club in eastern Iowa. These are all church people; yet their esoteric information has continually grown during more than thirty years of continual study! We who study beyond the traditional church doctrines also need to *cooperate,* rather than to *compete!*

This difference in interpretation is as old as the Pharisees, the Sadducees, and the Essenes. The latter were more or less "underground" in keeping the ancient truths from destruction, as were the Masons, Rosicrucians and other brotherhoods. They emphasized "knowledge" as much as "faith," and this came out in the Holy Bible. Luther called the book of James "an epistle of straw," because it emphasized "works" as a *result* of faith; whereas he emphasized the book of Romans which spoke a great deal about being "justified by faith" (Romans 3:28).

Which *is* more important, *Faith* or *Knowledge?* Faith without knowledge goes to many extremes, such as the snake cults that want to prove their faith by letting rattlesnakes bite them. But knowledge without faith becomes arid intellectualism, of which we have too much already in some quarters. An interesting side-light is that both Martin Luther and John Wesley were investi-gators of the psychic. Lutherans and Methodists seem chagrined when they discover this!

But "Knowing" meant something different to the Essenes. It was an "intuitive knowing" rather than something they read or heard from a lecturer. And "authorities" often fear such people; that's *why* they go underground. Usually these brotherhoods teach only what the pupil or "chela" can absorb: and they have ways of "knowing" how much that is. So one is not "initiated" until he becomes at one in purpose with the teacher or "guru."

Interestingly enough, the ruins of the Essenes' villages are still to be seen near the shores of the Dead Sea, and the "Dead Sea Scrolls" were discovered in one of the caves near there, where they had been put when the Essenes "knew" the Romans would devastate them as they had Jerusalem.

Some interesting coincidences surround this discovery. Those jars had probably been there for nineteen centuries, but it was not until 1947 that a shepherd boy "happened" to throw a stone in that cave and heard the jar break, whereupon he investi-gated. *That is the historic Year of the Flying Saucers!* And to make matters still more interesting, the place where some of these scrolls are now displayed is in an Israeli library *which is built in the shape of a flying saucer!*

HONESTY AND INTEGRITY

In this day and age when charlatans and "con men" abound, it is imperative that we stress these principles upon which civili-zation was founded! Fortunately the esoteric workers in Phoe-nix and surrounding area are not allowed to publicize their work or meetings unless they subscribe to a certain code of ethics. This code includes "helping people, not for our own ag-grandizement" and a "supportive attitude" toward others who subscribe to the same code. *Would that the whole Christian Church had such a code of ethics!*

Remember the "Law of Karma!" The Law of Cause and Ef-fect, or the Law of Compensation. In general, what you do to others will come back to you in some way. In this context see what the Golden Rule, often ascribed to Jesus only, says, "Do unto others that which you would that they do unto you." It is in the Old Testament, and in the Chinese, in different wording. Jesus preached this *and lived by it,* because of his "intuitive knowledge" of *this Law.* He said, "This *IS* 'the law and the prophets.' "

We had better get back to that law in our *Ecclesiastic,* our *Political,* our *Sociological,* and our *Economic* policies — or we will "reap the whirlwind" even more yet in the years to come! *Historic values are still in order, because "The Law" is still the same as it was!*

TRUTH IN COMMUNICATION

It is a rather well-known fact by now that much modern music has suggestive phrases in it regarding sex, the taking of alcohol and drugs, and other debilitating ideas. The beat itself is often erotic. What happened in popular media such as radio and TV and movies to the old classical music that lasted for *centuries?* What happened to the "easy listening" music of the forties and fifties, or even the better type of jazz? *Who was responsible for this "planned change" in our tastes?*

Music is a means of communication, whether it has words or not — and what has happened to young people's morals in the last thirty years answers the question as to whether these things "affect them" or not. Communication *does* affect us all.

The same might be said about other art forms which have taken on a pornographic trend — in art, itself, in "literature," in the movies and TV shows. Truth In Advertising legislation was necessary because we were being given false information about products we bought. And the Freedom of Information Act was also passed because many things were being supressed that had nothing to do with "national security."

I have seen some things that came from authors' requests under the Freedom of Information Act that still had many "censored" marks so that one could hardly read what *was* there. Many of these had to do with the Flying Saucers — which, as I stated before, has often been suppressed more by the United States government than by South American and other governments. Is this because they have the crashed saucer and the bodies?

Ray Palmer, along with Curtis Fuller, started *Fate* Magazine, the first issue of which Kenneth Arnold gave me. The magazine is still a favorite on the newsstands.

Palmer also started *Search, Mystic, Forum,* and *Flying Saucers,* and published such books as *Oahspe* with money his readers had loaned him. In some of these magazines, he had NASA satellite photographs. But when he started tying in *their own* pictures of the "holes at the pole" with Flying Saucers, he was removed from their mailing list, even though his was the best space magazine that anyone was publishing. And when Ray suddenly and mysteriously died while in Florida, Marjorie Palmer called me while I lived in Sioux City to have his funeral service in Wisconsin!

Jimmy Carter saw a flying saucer, and one of his campaign promises was that if he were elected president, he would release the government information on ·the subject.

Near the end of his presidency, I wrote him a straightforward letter asking why he had not kept that campaign promise. His office responded by simply having NASA send me an elaborate publicity magazine on their work, and in that magazine was about an inch and a half on the subject of UFOs!

So I wrote again, reminding the President's office that my question had not been answered, and repeating the request. The letter I received back from the "Director Of Presidential Correspondence" stated that "NASA had advised the President not to reopen formal investigations into reported unidentified flying objects at this time." This is one of many reasons for my having stated that "presidents are prisoners in the White House." It is obvious that they do not always make the decisions!

Then in a paragraph obviously designed to throw me off the track, it was stated that "although NASA to date has not received one piece of physical evidence for laboratory analysis, NASA officials are keeping an open mind on the subject."

Later I wrote President Ronald Reagan about the same subject, and I did not even receive a reply acknowledging my request. So a month or two later I wrote Nancy Reagan in hopes that I might by-pass the President's wary office. No acknowledgement from there either!

Since this is *not* a political problem of Democrats or Republicans, and the Air Force has publicly stated that it is *not* a matter of national defense, then *what is the reason the communication between "the people" and "their elected officials" is so evasive?* Did I hear someone say that I had previously mentioned MIRO?

Well, friends, if you want this to remain "the land of the free and the home of the brave," then let us awake to metaphysical principles whereby we can *all* communicate with one another by extra sensory perception. I am not joking by that remark! Do you now see why UFO occupants are communicating with thousands of private and "unknown" individuals?

Yes, *Truth in Communication* is a much-needed "traditional value," needed in *every* avenue of our society!

Hatonn, record keeper for the Galaxy Planet by his name where records are kept. © 1979 by Universal Mother Mary's Garden and the Mon-Ka Retreat, 116 Mercury Drive, Grass Valley, California 95945. (Artist - Celaya Winkler)

CHAPTER 21

Church-Anity versus Christianity

MANY PEOPLE have criticized the church over the centuries for one reason or another. There were times when it ruled all else with an iron hand. Everyone today knows what a telescope is and what it does. But there was a time when Galileo's telescope was condemned by the church as an instrument of the devil, and Galileo himself was threatened with excommunication if he did not recant some of his theories. The Earth was supposed to be the center of everything; therefore the Sun, Moon and stars revolved around the Earth! Surely God would not have sent his son to Earth unless it was *that* important!

Then came the Crusades, when, among other things, children died along the way to the Holy Land on an expedition that seems at this late date as "useless." And still later came the Inquisition, with its horrifying persecutions, murders, and destruction of property.

Today people point to the many shortcomings of the Church, and some of them are real! Many metaphysically-minded people leave the Church "because it does not give them enough spiritual food!" Others wander from one church to another, looking for a Spiritual Utopia. Many books have been published portending to show how much Truth the Church has covered up. Secret Service agencies do not have a corner on "cover-ups!"

A friend of mine likes to remind people that "Christianity has not failed; it simply never has been tried!"

William Dudley Pelley had his life turned around, after his imprisonment for trying to save America from the communist revolution here in America. He had a psychic revelation, when he actually talked to people whom he had known in the publishing field *before they died* — and this experience was *after* their death.

One of his "other-worldly friends" that he had known before told him to "remember what you did to get here, and you can return at any time." He did remember, and returned time after time.

The experience is related in one of his first Soulcraft Fellowship books, entitled *My Seven Minutes in Eternity with Their Aftermath*, a reprint from the epochal article published in *The American Magazine* for March, 1929. The book came out in 1956, the year I spent quite some time with Mr. Pelley at his "Box-factory Publishing House" and home in Noblesville, Indiana.

After this Mr. Pelley described the difference between Christianity and "Churchianity" in many of his magazine articles. It is from him that I derived the title for this chapter. He "remembered" his life with Christ in one of his dozens of books, as well as "returning to the heavenly world" again and again. Even long after Pelley's death there are clubs and study groups getting together to go through his many books and learn about the after-life and the "before this life." He was one of the pioneers in this "New Age Study," as was Edgar Cayce and the Cayce Foundation.

I have a series of very important articles in which Pelley describes, from a "re-embodiment standpoint," *why certain people come into this life to learn from one religion or another. In other words, the idea is to teach why millions of people incarnate as Moslems, and what they learn from that experience. Or as Hindus, and what there is to learn from that experience. The same with all the other religions of the world, especially Judaism and Christianity.

All one has to do is attend a dozen different denominations, or especially the "sects," to discover how wide is the disparity of beliefs in America — let alone the faiths of other parts of the world.

In my more than forty-five years in the ministry, I have run into my share of people who were sure their particular way of interpreting the Bible was the only correct one, and that anyone who disagreed was either going to hell (literally!), or at least to some sort of "purgatory" of their own definition.

This is what Pelley meant by "Churchianity," as opposed to

"Christianity." Actually, what these people need to be able to get a broader understanding of life and real Christianity is to be "born again" — and again — and again! And they will get that chance, if they don't broaden out here and now! Then someone else (for Pelley is in the Higher Dimensions) will probably write a series of articles on why one incarnates into a Catholic family, or a fundamentalist family, or a liberal Protestant family, or into a family of an off-beat sect — and what they can learn from each of those experiences.

In some cases the obvious lesson will come from the persecution that they have to endure from other belief-structures, because only in that way will they learn what they did to others when they were doing the judging and persecuting! "With what judgment you judge, you shall be judged." (Sermon on the Mount).

I have often wondered why the "Space People," who are communicating with thousands of people daily now, don't give us the final answers on all theological questions and settle the matter once and for all. But the great lesson in Genesis 2 and 3 is that man was given one of the greatest of all gifts — *Freedom.* He is not a robot! He has to learn in his own way, even by mistakes.

Christ (the "second Adam" — I Corinthians 15:45) came to correct the mistake of the "first Adam" who mis-used that gift of freedom. That gift of free choice is still operative. That's why the "Space People" cannot violate that law by interfering too much with the natural progression of any planet. So they do it just as God has always done it, not by direct intervention but by indirect means — intuitions, visions, dreams, etc.

CHAPTER 22

Some Typical Messages From Space

HUNDREDS OF people are now regularly receiving messages from space, since the government does not give us the messages *they* have received from the same source. It is most heartening to know about *the Guardians* at a time when our governments and news media seem to all be vying with each other to see who can scare us the most. We hope that it will be a message of *peace* to you at this time of more than a dozen areas of sanguinary conflict in the world.

I have received messages like the following from different sources who have no contact with each other — just with the same Source, *The Ashtar Command*. I have had contacts through other people with this Intergalactic Command for thirty years.

Francie Steiger's book reports that people continually keep getting the message, *"The time is now."* So we can wait no longer to give out these "Tidings of Peace!" This is a *typical* sample:

> *I am Ashtar, the Commander of ten million men surrounding this hemisphere in the protective force within the Alliance for Peace in the Intergalactic Council. We have called upon this messenger to compile this book (PROJECT: WORLD EVACUATION) for this point in earth time that mankind might consider and understand the details of those things that would come to pass, for "Our Father doeth nothing except first He warneth His*

prophets."
There is method and great organization in a detailed plan already near completion for the purpose of removing souls from this planet, in the event of catastrophy making a rescue necessary.

Ashtar here sounds a great deal like the "Rapture" that many fundamentalists talk about so much these days. They have felt for some time that *The Time is Now.* We continue with the Ashtar message of peace:

This book is not intended to frighten anyone, but on the contrary, to hold out the hope and confidence of our presence with you for any time of trouble. The dangers to the planet are very real. The resulting tragedy to humanity would be unavoidable. However, our presence surrounding you THIRTY-FIVE MILLION STRONG will assist you, lift you up and rescue you, and hold you in safety.

This protection is from many dangers! An asteriod collision, another solar system passing too close to the magnetic field of this one, or even a polar shift of this planet. They have been monitoring *many* things besides our *human intent!* That's probably why the UFOs pay scarce heed to those who "want to see one." They have more important things to do than to come to everyone who wants a demonstration.

There have been *plenty* of demonstrations. One that should have convinced the government, and probably did, was when they kept flying over restricted air space over our nation's capitol in Washington, D.C. in 1952. The surveillance of the above-mentioned types of danger is constant! More from Ashtar:

Now we take further steps, because of the shortness of time . . . This time WE DARE to expose our most secret strategy . . . we dare to expose our plans to come out into the open and send proof of our presence . . . to silence forever arguments and denials of our overshadowing protection . . . We dare to reveal (our representatives) and their identities, for no harm can come to them. We would simply remove them from your midst if you were to attempt to harm them in any way.
They are citizens of your planet, who have lived with

*you, suffered with you, walked with you and truly been one
of you. Now we call them forth to admit their identity, to be
gathered together to spend a brief time with us that they
might return to you and share with you the facts and the
proofs of our existence and the truths of our words.*

Kuthumi is a Master well-known to many people, along with
El Morya and Djwal Khul. They were the three Wise Men that
"saw his star in the East" and came to Judea "to worship him."
In a later lifetime Kuthumi was St. Francis. In *Climb the Highest Mountain* we read about him:

> *I would call to your attention the great depth of compas-
> sion which your blessed Kuthumi externalized in his em-
> bodiment as Saint Francis and which to the present hour
> in his ascended state remains an outstanding quality of
> this Master as he serves with beloved Jesus in the office of
> World Teacher. Truly his life was a message of God-com-
> passion for all Life.*

Kuthumi is still a guide to those who are doing outstanding
service to humanity at this time. Tuella is one of his "chelas,"
and she asked about the foregoing message from Ashtar.
Kuthumi explained:

> *Those who have come to your world and taken upon
> themselves the garment of flesh to serve the planet in Our
> Name, are approaching a time of crisis. These have chosen
> to be present upon Terra to serve in the great harvest of
> souls that now comes. To these, many instructions must be
> given, and many discussions sent to them to be assimi-
> lated within their guidance systems. Now is the hour when
> these special emmisaries are to be temporarily removed
> from Terra for a brief moment of time, to receive special-
> ized training instructions and personal directives, that
> they may be clothed in preparedness for the times that are
> at hand!*

These are typical of many messages I have seen, and I have
met several of their "representatives" who have been active a
whole lifetime on this planet already. They are now being contacted by their brothers and sisters of the stars!

CHAPTER 23

The End Times -
The Time of the End -
The End of Time

THESE ARE interchangeable terms in the minds of many people, indicating the "apocalyptic" end of history as we know it. Sometimes it is referred to as "the great day of the Lord," or just "the day of the Lord," or even just "the day." ("That day will not come, unless the rebellion comes first, and the man of lawlessness is revealed, the son of perdition." — II Thessalonians 2:3.)

All sorts of "apocalyptic" writings are in the Bible, in both Old Testament and New. And consequently this terminology has shown up in many Christian camp-meeting type songs, like: *When the Trumpet of the Lord Shall Sound, AND TIME SHALL BE NO MORE . . .*"

Many "liberal" Christians do not see anything but the continual ongoing of "history" as we have known it, and seem to dismiss such thoughts as these as just "apocalyptic writings" which try to describe a time of divine justice when "all things will be made right." Many "conservative" Christians take these words quite literally, and see every apocalyptic idea as an immediate change "in the twinkling of an eye" when Christ shall come in the clouds of the sky.

Without arguing either extreme, I would like to point out that there may be still another way of interpretation of these terms.

For instance, let us ask first, "What *is* time?"

Some would say "time is motion," and there is no time except as we move through space. *One day* is one rotation of the earth. The sun *seems* to come up every morning and go down every

evening. Actually the Earth rotates on its axis each day —
which is *movement*. When the astronauts in their capsule encircle the earth every ninety minutes, they have quite a few "sun-
rises" in each twenty-four hours. They need to look at the complex chronographs or watches they carry with them to note exactly what "day" it is, and "what time of that day" it would be
back at Cape Kennedy.

Likewise there is also the revolution of the Earth in an orbit
around the sun. One full revolution is *one year*. Six months after
one sees Orion or any zodiacal constellation in the night sky, it
is not there any more because we are on the opposite side of the
Sun, and there will be different constellations at which to look.
Any astronaut that could stay in a capsule as long as six
months would also have to know *where he was in space*.

It will add to the complication when we get to the time when
we can travel to Mars or Jupiter, for each has a larger orbit than
Earth, and therefore a "longer Year!" This will have to be taken
into consideration, for both Mars and Earth will have moved
during the trip, so *"Time"* will be different on Mars, and will certainly be different than on Earth. Calculations will have to be
made to determine even what *Month* it is on Earth while on a
trip to Mars!

So we are already approaching the time when (Earth) time
shall be no more, at least to a travelling astronaut. Such concepts were beyond the ken of most song writers who wrote about
"when time shall be no more," and beyond the imagination of
pre Copernican students of the stars who thought all of them
travelled around the Earth!

But there is another way to interpret "when time shall be no
more." Both concepts are either mind-boggling (to some) or at
least mind-stretching (to others). It is the "awakening" or the
"raising of consciousness" that so many New Age (Aquarian)
people are talking about.

This other interpretation takes in many of the concepts in
other portions of this book — "out-of-body" experiences (OOB);
communication with the spirit world (where their concept of
time is different from ours because *they are not limited by the
physical movements of the Earth* we have been describing, as
we are); mental telepathy with other physical beings on Earth;
the "changing of dimensions" of ships and people, going into
and out of visibility or invisibility and therefore into our world
(and our time) and out again.

Many people have had experiences, either in dreams, visions or meditative moods, when what seemed like a long series of things seemed to happen to them, but upon looking at the clock it was discovered that the whole long series of events had covered but a minute or two. One example I must quote verbatim happened to a lifelong friend of mine who chooses to remain nameless in my book:

> In the fall of 1943 while serving in the U.S. Army, we moved to Ft. Pierce, Florida. I took a weekend pass and by bus travelled to Winter Park, Florida, to visit with Dr. Brown Landone. I already knew that when the light was lit and the caller was in uniform of the U.S.A., the caller could just ring the bell, and someone would come to let him in. Dr. Landone had lost two sons in the 1898 war with Spain, and he understood war.
>
> Dr. Landone and I had quite a visit about things in general and about the American service men in particular. During a lull in our conversation I stooped to tie my G.I. oxfords, and in that short span of time the doctor and I carried on a conversation without any words being spoken aloud. Dr. Landone told me non-verbally about myself and about items that only I knew about. What I should do next was also a part of that unspoken conversation.
>
> So TIME does not seem to be a part of the future. NOW is the key to all the passing events.

He concludes:

> If it can be of any help in your book, use my rendition but do leave my name out, for each must find his own map of progress.

I have met many people who have had an out-of-body experience, some after an automobile accident, some in the hospital, and some while in a meditative mood. One who does not understand metaphysical principles sometimes believes he has "talked with God." Those who know better realize that "God has many Great Beings in His hierarchy" who do his bidding and seem to be God speaking. This misunderstanding is in many Old Testament passages where people "entertained" strangers, only to learn later that these visitors were *Angels of*

God. But if one reads the text carefully, there are times in the same passage where these "men" are called "angels" and just a bit later are referred to as "God." So there were mis-interpretations even among the ancients, either by the one having the experience or by the redactor who wrote them down at a later period.

I have also had correspondence with people who had "visited" ("out-of-body") a friend in another continent, seeing what that person was doing at a given moment. Upon writing to that person, mentioning the date, the time, and what she was doing, the reply astounded them both — for that is exactly what happened at that moment. People who have an OBE happen at "inopportune moments," notice that they are interrupting the privacy of that individual and quit immediately! "Spying" is not ethical in that realm any more than it is in the physical!

The point of this section is to speculate as to whether the "time of the end," the "end time," or the "end of time" has not already come for many people. If one enters "the twilight zone" *now*, where there is no time, then *Time Itself* has a new meaning for that person.

That is why "spiritual beings" cannot predict correctly the future *in our Time Zone*. And that is why the "physical beings" who enter that "timeless zone" cannot always tell how long they were there. *Time is no more for them* — while they are in that state of consciousness.

"Seeing into the future" is "seeing certain events which follow certain other events." But setting dates in our time zone is only an estimate, and not reliable; consequently, many people do not even believe that anyone can see into the future. But it happens all the time — to thousands of individuals so endowed with "spiritual gifts."

CHAPTER 24

Each Person Is Unique

I T IS OBVIOUS by now that this minister has had more unusual experiences in the ministry than most clergypersons, and why this book is so different from an autobiography by almost any other minister. I have felt very *alone* in my search at times; yet the Club I have mentioned over and over helped me to keep my sanity.

Why I have been chosen to have such a variety of experiences besides the usual ministerial experiences, I do not know. Could it have any connection with a vision I once had of being in the co-pilot's seat in a huge, wingless aircraft passing swiftly over the land, so close that I could see the ground? Whether this was an OOB experience or a fleeting memory of a past life I cannot say, but it remains as vivid in my memory today as on the day I had it! As does the vision (or OOB experience) I had of my master Jesus one night in the fall of 1936.

I do know that, in spite of criticisms from parishioners who were afraid I might be "influenced by the devil" in my research, Jesus remains my Savior and my Lord just as surely as that night I gave my heart to God at an altar in Hawkeye, Iowa, with my Mother at my side praying with me! *Each* transforming experience has been like a "born again" experience; and every time it happened, I had an exhilaration similar to when I gave my heart to God. My point in publishing this book is to give help and understanding to many along the way who have had experiences they cannot explain (and are afraid to talk about).

Another goal I have tried to keep in mind is that *each person is unique,* because no two people have had identical experiences throughout their lives. Therefore, *each one is on a different path from every other one,* and *no one should try to put anyone else in his own path, violating the God-given privilege of free will for everyone!*

A third goal, similar to the last-mentioned, is that we should stop judging the other's path. Metaphysical students, disillusioned with the Church, should remember where *they* were a quarter of a century ago in their search for truth, and *be able to see that the Church still answers many questions for many people!* And church people should stop stating that metaphysics is of the devil, or that their own denomination is superior to another's!

The Church was started on metaphysical principles, Jesus having practiced and taught them, but these principles have gotten lost along the way. Little by little, let us bring them back into the *only* institution that has publicly given these truths to the people, as fully or as meagerly as was possible at the time. "And the gates of hell have not prevailed against her" in twenty centuries! She has a world program of helping a hurting world! Let us simply add understanding that will make many of her truths more understandable and more palatable to more people!

This Epilogue is Prologue

T HE "CITY" detected by radar in the middle of this century, and which was revealed to John in his Revelation in the Holy Bible, must have been in the plans Jesus revealed to his disciples the last night of his life, as left to us in John's Gospel.

There are many dwelling-places in my Father's house; if it were not so I should have told you; for I am going there on purpose to prepare a place for you. And if I go and prepare a place for you, I SHALL COME AGAIN AND RECEIVE YOU TO MYSELF, SO THAT WHERE I AM YOU MAY BE ALSO. (John 14:2, 3 NEB)

Later he revealed to John how enormous this city was, its general description, and that some day it would descend to Earth (Revelation 21:1-27). Nothing unclean was to enter it — though the gates were continually open — no cowardly, faithless, vile, murderers, fornicators, sorcerers, idolaters or liars!

When I learned, from factual knowledge, in 1949, how the authorities were lying to us about the discs and the cigar-shaped ships that people were seeing and photographing, I remembered something else that Jesus said to his disciples on that last evening with them:

If you love me, you will obey my commands; and I will ask the Father, and he will give you another to be your Advocate, who will be with you forever — THE SPIRIT OF TRUTH. The world cannot receive him, because the world neither sees nor knows him; BUT YOU KNOW HIM, because he dwells with you and is in you. (John 14:15-17)

This explains as well as anything I can think of *why there is such confusion about this subject.* Spiritual things are spiritually discerned. But most of our earthly knowledge is *intellectual, and that's where we obtain most of our information.* Few are those who will accept *truth wherever they find it,* regardless of what it does to previous theories!

And this brings up a final note about Jesus' jurisdiction over *all* other Space Commanders. In the tenth chapter of the Gospel of John, verses 14 through 16 (NEB) we read Jesus' words on a previous occasion:

> *I am the good shepherd; I know my own sheep and my sheep know me — as the Father knows me and I know the Father — and I lay down my life for the sheep. BUT THERE ARE OTHER SHEEP OF MINE, not belonging to this fold, whom I must bring in; and THEY TOO WILL LISTEN TO MY VOICE. THERE WILL THEN BE ONE FLOCK, ONE SHEPHERD.*

This is exactly what is coming through from many Commanders, through many channels — they have come from far and near to help in the salvation of Earth, *and they are under the command of Jesus!* They come from the Higher Dimensions of Our Planet, Other Planets of our solar system, Other solar systems in our galaxy, the Milky Way, and even Other Galaxies.

When our puny knowledge, compared to theirs, talks about the "impossibilities" of traversing the distances involved — even if travelling at the speed of light — this shows again our earthbound, limited, *intellectural,* Piscean information. And those who are thus limited are finding the new Aquarian vibrations and information too much to swallow.

If we limit ourselves to Piscean information of yesterday, that's where we will stay. But if one "leads two lives," the practical one in which we live, and the vibrations of the space into which we are approaching, these concepts are accepted, a little at a time, but *faster and faster* "as The Day approaches," that "Great and terrible Day of the Lord."

I thought I "knew my Lord" when I accepted Him as my personal Savior at a tender age. But the more I learn, the more intrigued I am by the *stupendous knowledge* he had even during His incarnation here! And now *Salvation* means so much more in its total meaning than simply "saving my individual soul from hell!'"

> *From the information revealed to St. Paul, Romans 8:18-23 (RSV): I consider that the sufferings of this present time are not worth comparing with the glory that is to be revealed to us.* FOR THE CREATION WAITS WITH EAGER LONGING FOR THE REVEALING OF THE SONS OF GOD: *for the creation was subjected to futility, not of its own will but by the will of him who subjected it in hope;* BECAUSE THE CREATION ITSELF WILL BE SET FREE FROM ITS BONDAGE TO DECAY AND OBTAIN THE GLORIOUS LIBERTY OF THE CHILDREN OF GOD. *We know that the whole creation has been groaning in travail together until now; and not only the creation, but we ourselves, who have the firstfruits of the Spirit, groan inwardly as we wait for adoption as sons,* THE REDEMPTION OF OUR BODIES.

And from Alfred Lord Tennyson:

> *One God, one law, one element,*
> *And one far-off divine event*
> *TO WHICH THE WHOLE CREATION MOVES.*

So "do not be conformed to this world but be ye *Transformed by the Renewal of your Mind.*" (Romans 12:2)

Acknowledgements of Assistance in my Research For This Book

SOME OF those mentioned in the pages to follow have a higher credibility than others. I want the reader to realize this. My purpose in including so many people in so many fields of research is simply to show the extent to which I went in trying to find the truth of what is going on in and above this beautiful planet. Sometimes one has to put certain information "on the back burner" until either corroboration is found from other sources — or a more reliable source refutes what is found in a less reliable source. This I have tried to do faithfully.

I am quite aware of Paul's writings where, in Ephesians 2:2, he speaks of "the prince of the power of the air, the spirit that is now at work in the sons of disobedience." But we must also be aware of Jesus' words that after the powers in the heavens are shaken (atomic fission), then shall the Son of man "send forth the angels, and shall gather together his elect from the four winds, from the uttermost part of the earth to the uttermost part of heaven." (Mark 13:26, 27)

These strange sights in the heavens came in great numbers immediately after the 1945 atomic bombs and showed themselves "in clouds" and having "great power and glory" so that our "protective air forces" were powerless against them. Result: denial, debunking and debriefing (with stiff penalties for Air Force employees who told anyone anything else)!

For religious persons who fear other aspects of the New Age, regarding them as "the work of the devil," let me remind you of The prophecies of Joel. Peter quoted on the day of Pentecost from Joel 2:28, 29; but the footnote to Acts 2:17 in my Bible says "the gift of the Spirit to *all flesh,* and not just to chosen individuals (gathered together on that day), *is a mark of the Messianic Age.*"

My sincerest thanks go to *all* those who contributed to my own growth toward Christ-consciousness, even to those whose experiences warned me to be cautious in my approach to new knowledge.

PERSONAL INTERVIEWS, WHERE CONDUCTED, AND
APPROXIMATE TIME

Howard Rand, LL.B. (Member of Massachusetts and Maine Bars) — at
his home in Merrimac, Mass., in late '50's — American headquarters for
"Modern Israel" Studies.

Various Personnel at "Modern Israel" World headquarters, 6 Buckingham
Place, London, 1955. Bought several rare books there.

Various Personnel at Mt. Avalon, Glastonbury, England in 1970. This is
where the first Christian Church was built by Joseph of Arimathea, who, in
addition to providing the tomb for Jesus of Nazareth, travelled back and
forth to England where he owned tin mines. He built this church when the
persecution of Christians began in Jerusalem, taking several early disciples
of Christ with him.

Kenneth Arnold at his home in Boise, Idaho in 1949 and again in early
'50's. Arnold had pictures of the discs that flew over Mt. Rainier in 1947,
which were given to government agencies. Internationally known because of
this and other incidents, Arnold showed us irrefutable proof of the UFOs
existence, and that they flew ten times faster than anything we had at that
time. He gave me my first copy of *Fate* Magazine.

Ray Palmer, who, under another name, started *Fate* Magazine along with
Curtis and Mary Fuller. Palmer was an incessant publisher of "flying saucer"
information and had the largest saucer file in the world in the '40's. I was in
his home in Amherst, Wisconsin in 1950 or 1951, had correspondence with
him when a whole truckload of his *Flying Saucers* Magazine was confiscated
later. I was called to have his funeral in Wisconsin (which Curtis Fuller
attended), and a year later returned to marry his son.

Richard Shaver, widely known for his "Shaver Mystery" of the "tero" and
"dero" underground, and his prediction that "flying saucers would come." I
visited him at his home, where he was a neighbor to Ray Palmer in Amherst, Wisconsin.

George Adamski, at my home in Maquoketa, Iowa, around the early '50's.
He was one of the earliest (and most controversial) of the contactees, having
published pictures in his books of his trips on their "ships." He travelled and
lectured around the world, contacting European monarchs.

George Hunt Williamson and his wife, *Betty,* at our home in Maquoketa,
Iowa, in the early '50's. He had constructed plaster casts of the footprints of
the Venusian Adamski contacted in southern California, which casts we later
saw in the apartment of Desmond Leslie in London.

Desmond Leslie, in his London apartment in 1955 and later in Cedar
Rapids, Iowa, where he spoke to a large crowd. He is the nephew of Win-
ston Churchill, and co-authored Adamski's first book, *Flying Saucers Have
Landed* (1953). In the Cedar Rapids interview, he informed me that the
President Eisenhower contact by Space Commanders at Edwards Air Force
Base was most probably authentic, since he had talked to "high brass" that
were there.

Father Grasso at his apartment in Rome in December of 1954. He had written a treatise on the "flying saucers" with the "imprimatur" of his superiors on the front cover. The Pope at that time had already made a public statement (in U.S. newspapers) about what "The Church" would say and do about life on other planets, should there be any! I had been referred to Father Grasso by George Adamski, who "really got around!"

George King, Ph.D., early contactee, founder of the Aetherius Society, contacted by highly evolved "masters" on other planets. Interview with him on his speaking tour in the late '50's.

John Otto, in Chicago at a convention he sponsored featuring George Adamski in the middle '50's, and later in Maquoketa, Iowa. He was a well-known *early* researcher in the "flying saucer" field.

Dr. Charles Laughead, M.D. and his wife *Lillian,* in Maquoketa, Iowa, in the middle '50's and again in the late '50's in Prescott, Arizona, where he was employed at the Veterans' Administration Hospital.

Willard and Eunice Quennel from Detroit, early researchers in the same field. Also in Maquoketa, Iowa, in the middle '50's. Later we contacted them at their home in Phoenix (early '80's).

Richard Miller, in Maquoketa, Iowa, middle '50's. He and Williamson had been getting radio messages "from upstairs" by "tensor beam."

"Tuella" (Thelma Terrill), in Prescott, Az. in early '80's. She is a contactee and publisher of "space communications" (now of Durango, Colo.)

Dr. Edward Palmer (Rayonda) at his home in Portland, Oregon, once in 1979, and again at his home in 1984. Also in Seattle in July, 1984. His trip to the Moon in one of their space ships was written up in the *Journal of the Borderland Sciences Research Foundation* years ago.

Howard Menger of New Jersey, early contactee, in our home in Maquoketa, Iowa, in the middle '50's. (Author: *From Outer Space to You.*)

Dana Howard, early "saucer contactee" and psychic, at one of her speaking engagements in Iowa, middle '50's.

Buck Nelson, farmer from southeast Missouri, having had numerous contacts on his farm and went on speaking engagements dressed in overalls, at *their* suggestion. Interview in Davenport, Iowa, at a speaking engagement of his in late '50's, and again at his farm in Missouri in the '60's, where I saw the trees, still bent almost to the ground by the great weight of the ship which had landed there. He was often contacted by the F.B.I. and, strangely, by the Mormons from Salt Lake.

Rheinhold Schmidt, in Davenport, Iowa, in the middle '50's — *before* he had heard of Adamski or any other contactees. His experience of having been invited on board one of their "mother ships" where some of the crew spoke German is well known, both around Kearney, Nebraska, where this happened and on his speaking engagements around the country.

Daniel Fry and "Talilita," on his speaking engagements in the '50's.

Rev. Robert Short, early contactee, in his home in Joshua Tree, California in 1979, and again in Sedona, Arizona, in 1983.

Wayne Aho, who conducted "Flying Saucer conventions." I was keynote speaker at one in Kalamazoo, Mich. in the late '50's, and spoke twice at his

Seattle convention in 1984.

Irene Hughes, world-renowed psychic who "sees ahead into the future." Bible scholars call this "prescience," as in the case of Noah, Joseph of Egypt and countless others. Interviews at Spiritual Frontiers Conferences and at her office on Washington St., Chicago ('50's & '60's).

Jeanne Dixon, with gifts similar to Irene Hughes, advisor to President Roosevelt and writer of a column in the newspaper, Washington, D.C. Interview was in Omaha, Nebraska, where she had lectured a convention of oil men on what they could do to "clean up their act." (Late '60's.)

Ruth Montgomery, at a Spiritual Frontiers Fellowship Conference in Chicago, probably early or middle '60's. Famous writer, with Arthur Ford and others as her "guides."

Arthur Ford, famous psychic and minister of a mainline denomination, who "broke the Harry Houdini code" for Mrs. Houdini after Harry's death. In home of *Dr. Marcus Bach,* professor of religion at University of Iowa in the '50's, later at Spiritual Frontiers Conference in Chicago, still later at the First Methodist Church in Iowa City.

Neva Dell Hunter from Detroit, who started our search in the extra sensory perception field, and introduced us to Spiritual Frontiers Fellowship. Interviews in several homes, Maquoketa, Iowa, middle '50's.

Reginald Lester, psychic investigator from England, connected to the Church's Society for Psychic and Spiritual Study there, and connected with exorcisms of haunted houses and castles. Interviews in Sioux City, Iowa in the early or middle '60's.

William Dudley Pelley, movie producer of first *Hunchback of Notre Dame.* Later had undeniable visual and audible experiences with "dead" former associates in the writing and publishing fields. Author of *Seven Minutes In Eternity* and dozens of other books dealing with the psychic and reincarnation, a complete education in both fields. I spent many days interviewing him in his office and home in Noblesville, Indiana, in the years 1954-56.

Riley Crabb, editor of Borderland Sciences Research Foundation journals, which gave perhaps the first modern explanation of the "Unidentified Flying Objects" as coming from the invisible etheric worlds on this and other planets, and "lowering their vibrational rates" into our realm of visibility and audibility to give us warnings and protective information. Interviews in my home, Prescott Valley, Az., 1982-84.

Albert K. Bender, author of much information about "the Men in Black" and other "bad" experiences with U.F.O.'s and the psychic, probably due to his having surrounded himself in his home and surroundings with "scary" thoughts and materials. He finally closed down his research. I spoke with him in his place of business in Connecticut in the very early years of my research.

Stanley Matrunik, now of Apache Junction, Arizona. Psychic artist with chalk drawings of "people" he "saw" at his meetings. Interviewed at meetings of the "Cup and Saucer Club" in eastern Iowa, late '50's. (See text for the picture he gave me of my grandfather as he appeared to Stanley as grandfather had looked in a Biblical lifetime.)

Mark and Elizabeth Prophet, who, with the guidance of Master El Morya, started the "Summit Lighthouse" in Colorado Springs, Colo. Mark later "ascended" to be the Master Lanello now. Interviewed several times in Colorado Springs, and later in our home in Sioux City, Iowa (1962-65?) "Elizabeth" still carries on the masters' work in various places of the United States. Together they wrote *Climb the Highest Mountain.*

"White Bear" Fredericks, Hopi Indian, gave important information to Frank Waters for the book called *Book of the Hopi* about their background, legends and forecasts. I interviewed him and his wife Naomi in their apartment in Sedona, Arizona, in the early '80's.

Curtis and Mary Fuller, editors of *Fate* Magazine (of which I own the first copy, given me by Kenneth Arnold). They still publish stories of the true mystic happenings and individual experiences from all over the world. First interview in their offices in Evanston, Illinois in the middle '50's. Many interviews later at Spiritual Frontiers Fellowship Conferences and business meetings, as we were both on the national council of this organization.

Gray Barker, author and publisher of much UFO and related materials. Interviewed in a restaurant in his home town, Clarksburg, West Virginia, in the '50's. He was at that time interested in the "mothmen" and enormous monsters or robots.

George Van Tassel, contactee who was building the "Integretron" at the direction of Higher Beings he contacted at Giant Rock, California. Directions were as explicit as they were to Moses in regard to building the "Ark of the Covenant." Van Tassel had some definite opinions as to how Moses received *his* information about that and the tabernacle. We sponsored lectures by him in Sioux City, Iowa in the '60's. Also interviewed him and his second wife, Dorris, in their home in Yucca Valley, California in the late '70's or early '80's.

Brad Steiger, author of a hundred books and nearly two thousand articles. Interviewed him at his home in Decorah, Iowa, in the '50's or '60's. Later interviews included the home of Fay Clark in Perry, Iowa. In the '80's we were in the home of Brad and *Francie* in Scottsdale, Arizona.

Dr. (Rev.) Frank Stranges of Van Nuys, California spoke in our church at Maquoketa, Iowa in June of 1961. Later interviewed him in Phoenix, Arizona, in the '80's.

Michael and Aurora El Legion, interviewed in Phoenix in the '80's. I obtained the pictures of Masters and Space Commanders from them, which were painted as she "saw" them by Celaya Winkler of California.

Hugh Lynn Cayce, son of Edgar Cayce, interviewed at the headquarters of the Association for Research and Enlightenment (A.R.E.) in late '50's; He preached in our church in Sioux City, Iowa in the '60's. He held meetings in our home in the '60's. And we interviewed him again at an A.R.E. Convention in Phoenix, where we also interviewed *Dr. Bill McGarey,* M.D. and Mrs. *Dr. Gladys McGarey,* M.D. who operate a clinic in Phoenix based on the Edgar Cayce readings. The latter interviews in the '80's.

Scott Nearing and his wife from Maine are Christian socialists and experts in organic farming. They were in our home in Maquoketa, Iowa in the late '50's. (Socialist does *not* mean communist!)

CORRESPONDENCE WITH:

Major Donald Keyhoe, who in the early '50's was interested in information about the ten-mile-long ships seen in the atmosphere above Kansas at that time. Author of several U.F.O. books regarding the government's censorship.

Dr. Lincoln La Paz, astronomer. We corresponded about the green fireballs seen mainly in the Southwest, but some in the Midwest, often where UFOs had also been seen. This was in the '50's.

Rolf Telano (Ralph Holland), one of the Borderland Sciences associates in Ohio, about communications he was having with Space Intelligences in the early '50's.

George Adamski and *George Hunt Williamson* before and after we met. Adamski sent me photographs of the discs and mother ships that he had taken in the Nevada flats at the time of U.S. government atmospheric atomic bomb tests. Williamson corresponded regarding radio communications they had been having with the ships above. Our radio communication *from* "upstairs," "We find few on Earth yet ready" was sent to him, and this seemed to agree with the type of messages they were getting in Arizona. This was in the early '50's.

Since moving to Arizona from Iowa we have talked with a half dozen or more people who have either seen UFOs on the ground, been *physically* on their large mother ships, or communicated telepathically with Commanders of ships whose names I recognized from over thirty years ago.

In addition, people in my church in Arizona, who worked for NASA for seventeen years, have seen them several times hovering for a half hour at a time over our extinct volcanic crater in Prescott Valley. There seems to be continuing activity here (and perhaps elsewhere), although the newspapers hardly ever speak about it any more! The UFOs "program of enlightment of Earth people" seems to be in an entirely different phase in the last five to ten years.